KNOCKED UP BY THE SINGLE DAD

AN ACCIDENTAL PREGNANCY ROMANCE

LILIAN MONROE

∿

*If you'd like access to the Lilian Monroe Freebie Central, which includes bonus
chapters from all my books (including this one), just follow the link below:*

http://www.lilianmonroe.com/subscribe

Lilian

xox

1

ROSIE

"Come on, Harper, stay," I plead, holding out my hands in front of me. Harper's jacket is almost on. She's got one arm through the sleeve and is reaching for the other one. "The babysitter can stay a little bit longer tonight. It's my birthday."

"Yeah, Harper, stay." Jess says, standing next to me and staring at Harper. Both of us are a good six inches taller than her but she doesn't seem phased. Harper sighs and purses her lips at me, but I can see the smile in her eyes. She puts her hand up, pointing her finger at me.

"Fine. One more drink. But only because you're my best friend and my daughter's godmother."

"Yay!" I exclaim, wrapping my arms around my best friend. Ever since she had a kid she always smells like babies. It's a comforting smell, sort of fresh and homey at the same time.

"So, Rosie," Jess says as she waves the bartender over. "How does it feel to be another year older?"

"Feels like I was stabbed about six times," I respond.

They laugh, and then Harper looks at me with pain in her

eyes. I know she still blames herself for what happened to me, but she shouldn't.

A year ago, our ex-coworker kidnapped Harper and came after me. He held her hostage and came to my house and stabbed me in the chest and stomach six times. He was delusional and obsessed with Harper and thought I was trying to keep them apart. I was, in a way, but only as much as a someone trying to protect their best friend. He's locked up in a mental institution now, but it's still fresh in everyone's memory.

"At least you got some wicked scars," Jess says with a grin. I brush my hands over my rib, where the biggest jagged scar cuts across my body.

"They're fading now. You can hardly tell they're there," I say, glancing at Harper. Her face relaxes and she smiles back.

It's a lie, of course. When I was getting dressed this morning, I saw the same six angry red scars all over my chest and stomach. They mar my skin as a constant reminder of how close I came to death. I tug at the neckline of my shirt, pulling it up to make sure the scar above my heart is still concealed. It's become almost an unconscious movement now.

I smile at my best friend and she squeezes my arm in thanks. I know Harper is still struggling with the memories of it all even over a year later. I know she still struggles with being at home alone and with people coming up behind her. She hates surprises now. That's why I've never told her how much I've suffered over the past year, both physically and mentally. She has a new baby girl and she needs all the strength she can get. Besides, I can take care of myself.

Jess pulls me from my thoughts with a fresh drink, presented to me with a wink. I take it and smile, tucking a strand of my fiery red hair behind my ear before lifting the glass and tapping it gently against hers.

"You're far too serious for your birthday," Jess says. "This is the first time we've been able to celebrate in weeks. Months, even!"

"You're right," I respond with a smile. I shake my head and my red curls brush against my cheeks. I need to snap out of it. If not for my sake, for Harper's. It may be my birthday, but she deserves a night away from the baby.

"We need to find you a man, is what we need to do," Jess announces. She spins around, surveying the room like an expert judge. I laugh.

"That's the last thing on my mind right now."

Jess shoots me a look and rolls her eyes. "Don't lie to me, Rosie."

The three of us laugh and Harper pokes me in the ribs with her elbow. I throw up my hands. I haven't been out in months and haven't had sex in who knows how long. Call it residual fear of people, or stress, or whatever. I've just been saying I'm busy with work, but the thought of letting a strange man into my apartment still makes me uneasy. Ever since the incident last year I haven't been the same.

"Fine. Fine. Yes, I need to get laid. But I'm not going to jump into bed with just anyone."

Jess turns those dark brown eyes toward me. She lifts an eyebrow and even though she looks sarcastic I know it's coming from a place of love.

"Rosie, not only do you need to get laid, you need to get royally Fucked with a capital 'F'."

Harper laughs and I can't help but join in. I shrug and nod my head, giving in. Jess dips her chin and turns back toward the bar.

"Now, who's going to be the lucky man," she says almost as if she's speaking to herself. She taps her fingers against her chin and swings her eyes around the room.

"Come on, Jess, don't force it," I laugh.

"What about him?" She says, pointing across the room.

"Can you *be* more obvious?" I protest, laughing. Her arm is extended and she's pointing straight at a group of men. "No. Definitely not," I say after glancing at the man. He looks over at us and our eyes meet for an instant. My cheeks immediately start burning. I look away and stare at Jess with my eyes wide. She grins.

"Okay, fair enough. I don't like his shirt anyway. What about him?" She asks again, pointing to another man.

Harper laughs. "Or him?" Now she's pointing to another man, both of them grinning from ear to ear.

I swat at their arms, laughing. "Guys, stop."

"Well it's never going to happen with that attitude," Jess says with an exaggerated eye roll. She cracks a smile and shrugs, turning back to her drink. "You're destined to be an old maid. I'm just trying to help."

"Nothing wrong with being independent," I respond, relieved that she seems to be distracted for now. I have no doubt she'll be back on the prowl for me in a few minutes. "I'm going to get us some drinks."

I breathe a sigh of relief when they let me go, still laughing and glancing around the room. I know for a fact there isn't a man in here I want to sleep with tonight, but I'll play along for now.

2

ROSIE

I SLIDE my way to the bar and try to catch the bartender's eye. I lean over and glance toward him, ready to tell him my order. I'm so focused on getting an opportunity to order that I don't see the man slide in beside me until he speaks.

"Buy you a drink?" He asks in a low growl. I almost jump out of my skin and whip my head around. It's the man with the awful shirt that Jess was pointing to. Great.

"No, I'm okay, thanks," I respond, turning back toward the bar.

"I saw you staring at me earlier."

My spine stiffens. I already said no, and here he is still talking to me. I swivel my head slowly and stare at the man. He's got dirty blond hair and his shirt is a short-sleeved muddled brown and green plaid. He's got one too many buttons unbuttoned and I can see his unruly carpet of chest hair. It truly is one of the most revolting shirts I've ever seen.

"First of all, I wasn't staring. My friend was just commenting on your shirt. Second of all, I told you I'm not interested. Please leave me alone."

"My shirt?"

My jaw almost drops. Once again, this guy has ignored my blatant comment about not being interested. He's more concerned about his shirt than he is about the fact that I told him to leave me alone. I feel that familiar sense of panic rising in my throat.

Ever since the incident last year, strangers stress me out. Unfamiliar places stress me out. I glance around at my friends and see Jess and Harper deep in conversation. The man is still staring at me and the faint stench of his body odor starts making its way to my nostrils. My heartbeat is getting faster and faster as I turn back toward the bar.

"You were saying something about my shirt? What's wrong with it?"

My fear intensifies. He's not leaving me alone. I can almost feel the scars on my chest starting to burn, like a beacon warning me of danger.

This is why I don't go out. This is why I don't talk to strange men. They just can't take no for an answer and I'm left feeling vulnerable. The words catch in my throat and my body stiffens even more.

"You got those drinks yet?"

Jess's voice is the best thing I've heard in my life. It's like a lifejacket when I'm about to go under. She slides in between me and the man and turns her back to him. I glance over her shoulder and see the beginning of anger in his eyes, and I pray that he's not the type to get upset. I turn back to Jess.

"No, not yet. The bartender is pretty busy."

She nods and waves her hand. Within seconds, she has our drinks ordered and paid for. They arrive a minute later and we grab them, heading back toward Harper.

"What was that about?"

"He came up to me at the bar and asked why I was staring at him. I told him I was staring at his shirt and to leave me alone but he wouldn't take a hint," I respond. My heart is still pounding in my chest.

Jess puts an arm around my shoulder. "I'm sorry, Rosie. I was just trying to have a bit of fun. If you're not ready to be with a guy then you're not ready."

She hugs me and Harper puts her arm around me too. "We're here for you. However long it takes you to feel comfortable around people is fine. The fact that you're out in a bar is a big deal."

I feel tears gathering behind my eyelids. "Thanks, Jess. I just don't think I'm ready to let a man into my house or into my life. I still start freaking out whenever someone talks to me."

She squeezes my shoulder and Harper clears her throat. Her eyes are filling with tears. I shake my head as a pang passes through my heart. The last thing I want to do is make Harper feel bad about it.

Jess shrugs. "I wouldn't worry about it, Rosie. His shirt truly is one of the ugliest things I've ever seen. It was even worse up close." She takes a sip of her drink and I start chuckling. Harper cracks a smile and Jess brings her drink down again. "And that chest hair! God. At least a trim. I'm not a fan of waxed chests, you know, I like a bit of chest hair on a man but even I have my limits."

Jess shakes her head and now both Harper and I are laughing. My shoulders relax and I let the air out of my lungs. I know I was overreacting, but both Jess and Harper understand. Harper starts telling us about her daughter and the panic inside me dissipates completely. I know there won't be any more talk of men or getting laid tonight, and I'm glad.

3

LUCAS

"You sure you don't want to come out? It's your last night."
Max is looking at me expectantly, one eyebrow raised as he
gauges my reaction. I try to smile but I think it might look like
a grimace.

"Nah, I'll just take a cab to the hotel. Early flight
tomorrow."

Max shakes his head and grabs his jacket. "Your loss,
man. There's a lot of great women in New York City."

"Thanks, Max. I'm just tired tonight. Want to hit the
ground running with this stuff when I get back to LA." I wave
my hand across my desk at the neat stacks of paper that are
ready to be packed into my bag. Max shrugs.

"Alright, well I'm going to head out. We'll be in touch later
in the week for the launch."

"Have fun," I say as Max turns around and walks out. I
sigh in relief. I couldn't think of anything worse than going
out drinking tonight. His promise of 'great women' just makes
me think of loud bars and loud women and people rubbing
up against each other. I haven't met any 'great women' since

my wife died, and I'm not sure they exist anymore. I just want to sleep.

I rub my eyes and run my fingers through my hair. My body is aching and I haven't even been to the gym all week. It was supposed to be a short business trip, over and back in two days, but it's stretched out to ten days, twelve to fourteen hours in the office every day.

We're launching my client's new music album in a week, and Max's advertising firm is the best in the country. I glance at the advertisement mockups and the schedules laid out in front of me and take a deep breath. The next few weeks will be completely manic, but they're crucial if we want this album to top the charts.

My phone buzzes and I smile as I see the name pop up.

"Hey kiddo," I say into the receiver.

"Dad, I got 98% on my math quiz today!"

"Wow," I smile. "That's incredible, Hon!" I mean it too. I lean back in my chair and listen to my daughter as she tells me about her day. I smile and close my eyes.

"So you're going to be back tomorrow?"

"Yep, tomorrow afternoon. Can't wait to give you a big hug, Allie."

"Me too." Her voice is full of energy. "I have a surprise for you!"

"A surprise?" I answer. "What is it?"

"I can't tell you, then it wouldn't be a surprise."

I feel my shoulders relax and the smile spread from my face through my whole body. Ten days was far too long to be away from my little girl. She giggles and I feel that familiar warmth spreading in my chest whenever she makes me laugh.

"Okay, I have to go, kiddo. I have to pack and get ready for my flight. I'll see you tomorrow."

"See you tomorrow, love you Dad."

"I love you too, Allie."

We hang up and I sigh. Hearing her voice was exactly what I needed. Whenever I feel like I'm too focused on work she always reminds me of what's important, and tomorrow I get to see that little grin and kiss her cheeks. I stand up and start stacking my files. I slip them into my briefcase and then pack up my laptop.

I flick off the lights and look back at my temporary office. Hopefully I won't have to be back here for a long time. I'll get this album off the ground and take a few weeks off to spend with Allie.

When I step outside, the cool night air hits my face and I fill my lungs. I take a deep breath and smile. I'll be back home tomorrow.

I glance up and down the street and frown when I don't see a cab. I turn toward the nearest main road and let my feet take me there as my mind wanders back to LA, to our little house in the suburbs and to Allie's smiling face.

Ninety-eight percent, I think as I shake my head. She's smarter than her old man, that's for sure. I smile and turn my head just as a cab turns down the street. Perfect. I extend my hand and watch as he puts his indicator on and starts to pull over.

I glance down and see my shoe is untied. I wave at the cab until it starts to pull over and then bend over to tie my shoelace. I hum to myself as I tie my shoe, not paying attention to anything except the lightness in my heart. I'm going home, finally.

I hear a car door slam and I glance at the cab. He's still there, so I stand up and start jogging over to it. Just a few more hours and I'll be with my little girl and out of the chaos of New York City.

4

ROSIE

"SEE you in the morning for brunch!" I call out as Jess and Harper head off in the opposite direction as me.

"Definitely," Jess answers with a grin. "Maybe the waiter will be hot and you'll have more luck getting laid tomorrow." She winks and I roll my eyes, laughing. She's relentless. I hope the waiters are all women and I won't have to deal with her jokes all day tomorrow. One night interacting with strangers was more than enough.

I turn back toward the street and wince as I take a step. My feet are aching from these ridiculous heels. My apartment is only a fifteen minute walk away but I might have to take a cab. It is my birthday, after all. I can be a little bit lazy tonight, of all nights.

I glance toward the street and sigh as I see a cab turning down toward me. I raise my hand and smile as the cab puts his indicator on and slows toward me. Perfect timing. I open the door and sigh as I sit down, easing the pressure on my feet. They're throbbing and I exhale as I slip my feet out of the heels. They definitely weren't this tight when I put them on a couple hours ago.

"Hi, can I go to—"

Before I can finish my sentence, the other back door opens and someone slips in. I immediately inhale his fresh, spicy scent and feel a warmth spreading in my core. The feeling surprises me and I can feel myself flushing as I realize what I'm feeling: the first stages of desire. That quickly turns to outrage as the man starts to speak to the driver.

"Hi, the Hilton by the airport, please." His voice is deep and smooth. Before I can protest, the cab driver nods his head and starts moving.

"Excuse me," I start. "What are you doing?" The warmth inside me turns to anger and indignation as I realize he's trying to steal my taxi.

The man turns his eyes to me and I'm almost knocked back. His face is chiseled with just a hint of stubble over his strong jaw. His eyes are a piercing blue and he stares at me with a complete calm.

"I'm going to my hotel. What are you doing in my cab?"

"*Your* cab? I was very clearly in it first."

I see the cab driver glance at us in his rear-view mirror and frown.

"You two don't know each other?"

"No," we answer in unison. I almost yell it, and the stranger says it as if it's a joke, as if the smile is playing just behind his lips. I shoot a glance at him sideways and feel something stir inside me when I see he's still staring at me. I push the feeling down and focus on my anger. The cab driver slows to a stop.

"So where am I goin'?"

"As soon as this man gets out, I'll give you my address," I respond, raising an eyebrow toward the door next to him. There's no way I'm saying where I live with him in here. He keeps his eyes on me and lifts his eyebrow in response.

"I'm not going anywhere. I was waiting for a cab on that street for ages. I have a flight to catch in the morning."

"Well, you're not staying here. You can't just jump in a taxi that's already been taken."

A smirk plays over his lips as his eyes travel down my body. I feel a shiver travel down my spine as his eyes take in every inch of me. Why do I like this feeling? I should be angry.

"How about this," he starts. "We drive to your place first, drop you off, and then I keep going toward the airport. We both get where we need to go, and I'll cover the fare."

I desperately want to say yes. His smell is intoxicating and I can hardly think straight with those eyes all over me. *Okay,* I think. *That sounds alright.*

"No."

He smirks again and I'm simultaneously annoyed and entranced.

"Why not?" He asks almost innocently.

"Yeah, why not?" The cab driver chimes in. We both ignore him, our eyes locked on each other. His question hangs in the air between us as the seconds tick by. I can't look away. His blue eyes drill into me and all I want is for him to look at me again. He licks his lips and the warmth in my core blossoms.

"Fine," I concede. The man's smirk spreads to a smile and he nods.

"Great. Where to?"

I sigh and give the cab driver my address. Sitting back in my seat, I stare straight ahead and try to ignore the pounding of my heart against my ribcage. My whole body is screaming at me to turn my head, to glance at him again. I can just see him in my peripheral vision, and it's taking every ounce of willpower to stop myself from looking at him.

He clears his throat and I close my eyes, trying to ignore the shiver that every sound and every move sends down my spine. I've definitely had one too many drinks. This feeling is not normal.

"Sore?" He asks softly.

I can't help it. I turn my head toward him and frown. "What?"

He nods to my feet. My shoes are off, my feet resting gently on top of them. I feel myself blush. I'm that typical drunk girl on her way home from the bar. I didn't even have that much to drink!

"Yeah."

I can't think of anything else to say. I can hardly think of anything except the throbbing between my legs growing to an ache whenever his eyes pass over me. Maybe Jess was right. I do need to get royally Fucked with a capital F if some stranger has this effect on me.

Still, when I look at him, I can't help but feel like he isn't just 'some stranger'. I haven't felt this comfortable around a man since before the incident with Harper's stalker. Usually I'd be nervous just being around a stranger, let alone saying my address in front of him. There's just something about him that makes me feel at ease. Maybe it's the way he's looking at me. There's a kindness in his eyes that makes me want to be near him.

"Here," he says in a low growl, holding out his hand. I don't understand so I just stare at him. He smiles more softly this time. "Give me your foot."

"What? I..." my voice trails off as his eyes bore into me. As if out of my control, I watch my leg shift and my foot lift up toward his waiting hand.

The instant my skin touches his hand it's like an electric current travels straight up my leg toward my center. The heat in my core intensifies and I feel my panties starting to soak through as his hand moves over my foot in slow circles.

I want him. My head is spinning. It's as if my body has a mind of its own and I'm just along for the ride.

I close my eyes and lean back. His touch is gentle at first, rubbing my heel and the arch of my foot. He uses both hands, completely covering my foot as he rubs it in smooth, long motions. My whole body relaxes as he moves his fingers up my arch toward my toes. I let out a soft groan and he chuckles.

The sound snaps me back to myself. I tense up and take my foot away, slipping it back into my shoes. I clear my throat and sit up, smoothing my dress down in front of me.

"That's okay, you can stop here," I say quickly. "I'll get out here."

"We're still five minutes away," the cabbie starts.

"That's okay, I'll get out."

"Whatever, lady," he says under his breath as he pulls over. I practically jump out of the cab and stumble toward the sidewalk, heart thumping and breath ragged. I vaguely hear the man yell out behind me but all I can do is rush down the street toward my apartment.

What. Just. Happened.

5

LUCAS

"Wait," I call out right before she slams the door. "Wait!"

I throw some money over the cab driver's shoulder and dive out of the car, grabbing my bag and cursing how heavy it is. She's just down the street, jogging as fast as her heels will take her. Her red hair is trailing behind her like a blaze and I can't keep my eyes off her.

"Wait! Hold on."

She stops dead and whips around to face me.

"What?" She pants. "What do you want?"

I come to a stop a few feet away from her. Her chest is heaving up and down and her eyes are bright green, shining brightly in the moonlight. I can't help it. I'm drawn to her. I don't just want to massage her foot, I want to touch every inch of her skin. I want to wrap myself around her and smell her, taste her, touch her until I know every detail of her body. The tiredness I felt just a few minutes ago has evaporated. I need to know who this woman is.

"What do you want?" She asks again, more softly this time. Her eyes are still blazing. I open my mouth and close it back up again.

"I... I don't know," I respond lamely. I hold my arms out and then let them drop to my sides. "Your name, for a start."

Her eyes narrow. "No."

"No?"

"Why would I tell you my name? You jump in my cab and convince me to let you ride along. You somehow end up giving me a foot massage and now you're following me down the street? I should be running away as fast as I can right now."

Her words are harsh but her voice has something else to it —amusement, or curiosity. Hope spreads through my chest. Maybe I have a chance with her.

"So why aren't you?" I ask, taking a step toward her. My body is vibrating, buzzing with anticipation. I've never seen a woman like this before. Her fiery red hair bounces in curls around her face when she shakes her head. She puts her hands on her hips and I can't help but drag my eyes along the curve between her waist and her hips.

She doesn't answer my question, so I take another step toward her, flicking my eyes up toward hers. She doesn't move.

"Don't you have a flight to catch?" Her voice is a breathy whisper and she's completely still.

"Not till the morning." I take another step forward. I can feel the vibration of her body. She's like a coiled spring, and she's just as tense as I am. I take a deep breath in through my nose, keeping my eyes steady on her face. She bristles as I take a step forward but stands her ground. We're inches apart.

I move slowly, lifting my hand toward her waist. My fingers just brush the thin fabric of her dress and she closes her eyes, letting a soft breath out of her mouth. I put my hand on her waist and slide it around toward her back. Her spine dips in down the center of her back and brush my fingers along it, down toward the curve right above her ass. My other hand finds her hip and she finally melts, trailing her fingers up my arms and opening her eyes.

"Who are you?" she whispers.

"I'm Lucas," I respond just as her fingers find the nape of my neck. I shiver as her skin touches mine and I can't wait any longer. My chin dips down and I crush my lips against hers. The tension in my body explodes. I pull her into me, sinking my fingers into her flesh and gripping her tightly. She tangles her fists into my hair and pulls me down for a deeper kiss.

Calling it a kiss is wrong. It's more than that. This is pure passion in physical form. She tastes sweeter, better, softer than I could ever imagine. My fingers find that curve in her spine and run up toward her neck, pressing her body against mine. Her breasts are pressed against my chest and I can feel my cock pulsing in my pants.

My body is out of my control. I've never met a woman who has this effect on me. She drops her hands to my shoulders and digs her nails into me. The pain is sharp but it fades quickly and sends a thrill straight down my spine. My cock pulses in response and she presses herself against it. She makes that soft moaning sound again and the throbbing between my legs intensifies.

I drop my hands toward her ass and she grinds herself against me, moaning into my lips again. I catch the moan with my mouth and it tastes just as sweet as her kiss.

A voice pulls me out of my trance. Someone brushes past us and yells back at us in a typical New York accent.

"Get a room." The gruff, angry voice grates against my ears and jolts me back to the world around me.

Rosie pulls away and glances back toward the man who

keeps walking briskly away from us. She looks back at me and giggles, bringing her hand up to her lips. Her nose crinkles a little bit and she flicks those bright green eyes back up at me. I smile.

"Oops," I say. "Got a bit carried away there."

"Come on," she says softly, slipping her hand into mine. "Let's go to my place."

I can't say anything in response, just let my footsteps fall in beside hers. My heart is thumping and I'm afraid she'll change her mind. I glance at her as she brushes a strand of hair and tucks it behind her ear. She looks over at me, catching me staring. She smiles and squeezes my hand gently.

"I'm Rosie," she says with a wink. "I guess you're allowed to know that now."

I smile and nod. "Nice to meet you."

She smiles and I watch her dip her head down and then glance back up at me. All I can do is pray that this night never ends.

6

ROSIE

THE INSTANT MY DOOR OPENS, we're stumbling in, arms wrapped around each other and hands clawing at clothing, bodies, hair. It's frantic. I can hardly breathe but I know that all I want is him. I've never felt anything like this before. It's like my body knows him already, and knows that I need him. I'm drawn to him and every time he touches me it sets my body ablaze.

I fall onto my sofa and he's on top of me, kissing my lips, my chin, my neck, my ear. His lips are soft and I feel his tongue slide out and taste my skin. He groans.

"You taste so good," he breathes.

"So do you," I reply, staring down at his face. He smiles and shifts himself back up to kiss my lips. I tangle my fingers into his dark hair and pull him closer, grinding my hips up toward him. I can feel his hard cock trapped in his pants and it makes my body ache with desire. I've never wanted anyone, or anything, as much as I want him right now.

The fear I felt at the bar has evaporated. The uneasiness that's plagued me since I was attacked is gone, and all I feel is lust. I want him.

I press my hips up toward him and Lucas groans again, sending yet another thrill straight through my center. I love the noises he makes. His hand slips across my shoulder and finds my breast, squeezing it gently as he grinds his hips down toward me.

I'm soaking wet, and I still have all my clothes on. As if he can sense my desire, he slips his hand down from my breast, trailing his fingers down my stomach and over my hip. He finds the hem of my dress and slides his hand underneath it. His touch is warm and heavy as he slides his hand back up my thigh.

Thank God I shaved this morning, I think as his fingers run along the outside of my thigh. He finds my hip and traces the bone over toward my pelvis. My center is throbbing and my heart is pounding against my ribcage. I know my panties are completely soaked as his fingers inch closer toward them.

He slides his hand over my panties and places his palm between my legs. He groans into my neck and kisses my skin.

"You're soaked," he breathes.

"I know," I reply. "I can't help it."

"Why would you want to?" He replies as he lifts his head and places another kiss on my lips. I wrap my arms around him and breathe in deep as he kisses me again and again. His hand slides over and back between my legs and the fire inside me intensifies. His palm is warm and I desperately want to feel his skin against mine.

Reading my mind, he slips his fingers under the edge of my underwear, tracing the hemline all the way up to my hip. I whimper.

"Stop teasing me."

He lifts his head up and grins, eyes shining. His fingers slip back down along the hem, so close to my slit but just brushing the edge of it. "Where's the fun in that?"

"I want you."

"I know," he says. "I want you more than I've ever wanted anyone."

His words pass through my body and my entire being vibrates with desire. "So take me," I breathe. "Fuck me, Lucas."

The words are like a switch. The second they leave my mouth his eyes change from desire to pure animal instinct. He growls and wraps his fingers around my panties and rips them down my legs. I gasp and then giggle.

"Careful! Those are my nice pair."

"Your nice pair, wow, what's the occasion?" He grins.

"It's my birthday," I answer. He cocks his head to the side.

"Seriously?"

"Yeah. Birthday undies. Or something."

He laughs. "I'll get you new ones," he says with a smirk as he rips them down my legs again. I kick them to the side and let my legs fall open. He groans again as his eyes are drawn between my legs. I bite my lip, suddenly shy. He shakes his head and glances at my face before dipping his head down.

The instant his lips touch my slit it's like a thousand explosions going off at once inside me. His tongue twirls and he devours me, moving his head up and down between my opening and my bud. I moan, tilting my hips up toward him as his arms wrap around my legs to hold them open. I reach down and run my fingers through his hair, making a fist and pressing down gently. He groans and kisses me harder, tasting me like I've never been tasted before.

"Lucas," I breathe.

I don't even know what I want to say. I want to tell him how I feel, but how can I put it into words? I want to tell him his tongue is magic, his touch is making me drunk, his groans are vibrating through my whole body but all that comes out is another moan. I want to tell him that for the first time in a year, I don't care about what's going on outside. I'm not listening for footsteps and I'm not looking over my shoulder.

I'm here, right now. Nowhere else. Just me and him. There are no words for this feeling. His arms squeeze my legs and spread them wider and he dips his tongue into my opening.

It's not enough. I want more. I want *him*. I want him to plunge his cock so far inside me it feels like he's piercing through me. I want to feel his shaft throbbing as he drives himself into me and grips my body with his hands. I want to feel every inch of him inside me and I want to grab onto his body like it's my only lifeline.

I run my fingers from his head to his jaw and say his name again. It comes out as a hoarse whisper. "Lucas,"

He pulls his lips away from me and I watch as he licks my glistening wetness off them. I gasp.

"Fuck me," I plead. His lips curl up into a grin and he lets go of my leg. He drags his finger through my wetness and then closes his eyes as he licks the taste. His groan makes my heart jump in my chest and I squeeze my thighs toward him.

"Fuck me," I whisper again.

"If you say so," he growls.

7

LUCAS

THERE's something intoxicating about a beautiful woman saying something profane. Maybe it's the way her lips move when she says the words, or the way her eyes blaze. Maybe it's the way her voice is barely louder than a hoarse whisper, or the way her hips grind into me just as she says it.

Whatever it is, as soon as those two little words come out of her mouth, I'm ready to explode.

Fuck me, she says, and my cock almost bursts through my pants. It's painful. I stand up and my hands tremble as I try to undo my belt buckle, jiggling it and sliding the belt out of the hook.

"I'll kill the man who invented the button fly," I say as I struggle with my pants. Rosie laughs and helps me unbutton my pants.

"Maybe it's just an excuse to ask for help," she says with a grin as her fingers undo the last button.

She's touching my stomach, running her hands under my shirt to feel my chest. I groan and drop my pants. Her hands fly to my crotch. With only the thin fabric of my boxers between her skin and mine it's almost too much to bear.

I reach down and lift up her dress, sliding it up her abdomen.

"What's this?" I breathe as a jagged red scar comes into view. I glance up at her and she looks away, pushing her dress back down.

"It's nothing."

I sit down on the couch and gently run my fingers under her dress, over her stomach and around her waist. I dip my head down and kiss the crease between her hip and her crotch, pressing my lips gently as I inhale her scent. I move my lips a little bit higher as I push the fabric of her dress upward. Her hands relent, letting me explore another inch or two of her stomach.

The edge of the scar comes into view and I press my lips against it. I feel her tremble and shiver underneath me and I kiss it again. Her body tenses and I run my fingers up her side. She relaxes and sighs and I kiss her again, pushing her dress up a little bit further.

She shifts her weight and I slowly peel her clothes off over her head. As soon as it's off she crosses her hands over her chest. Her eyes are searching my face, she looks nervous, or embarrassed. I let my eyes drag down from her face over her chest and stomach. I count the scars as I touch them, just barely grazing my fingers over them.

"Six," I breathe. I glance at her face and see her eyebrows knit together. "You're gorgeous," I say and her eyes dart back to mine. I look back at her stomach and dip my head down to the first scar I saw. "One," I start, kissing my way all along the length of it. Her body relaxes a little bit under me. "Two," I continue, moving to the next scar. Her body relaxes a little bit more. "Three."

I keep going until I've covered every scar with my lips. Rosie sighs and I bring my lips up to hers.

"You're gorgeous," I say again. Her lips finally curl up into a shy smile.

"Smooth talker," she says. I shake my head. I wish I could let her know that this isn't how it is, this isn't how I am. This is something special.

Instead of responding, I crush my lips against hers and let my weight cover her body. My cock is straining against my underwear harder than ever before, and Rosie wraps her legs around my waist. I can feel the heat of her center pressed up against me. I can't wait any longer.

I rip my underwear down my legs and reach down to my pants to grab a condom. My cock is rock hard and Rosie reaches down to wrap her delicate fingers around it. She strokes it gently as I rip the crinkling package open and take the condom out. I groan and then roll it over my hard cock. Rosie shifts her weight and lifts her eyes up to mine. She stares at me through her lashes and a devilish grin paints itself on her lips. I grin back and grab my cock, positioning it against her and pausing for just a second.

Entering her is indescribable. It's ecstasy. It's unadulterated pleasure. It's incredible. My eyes close and the breath escapes my lungs as I push in slowly, feeling her walls adjust to my girth. When I feel my cock hit the depths of her pussy, I open my eyes and she gasps. Her eyes are wide and she's staring at me. Her hand reaches up and she places it over my chest, over my heart. I interlock my fingers over hers and reach down to grab her breast.

I try to keep my strokes long and slow but before I know it, I've lost control. She's moaning and digging her fingers into my skin and I'm driving my cock deep into her. I thrust deeper and harder and drop my chest down so that I can kiss her again.

I drive my cock into her and crush my lips against hers,

tangling my fingers into her fiery red hair as she moans into my mouth with every thrust.

Our bodies are completely connected. She takes my cock inside her and grips it tightly as I push myself into her. Her legs squeeze my waist, and I groan as I feel her contract around me. Her whole body starts to tense as her back arches. I can feel the pressure building inside her just as it's building in me and I reach down to find her bud.

My thumb makes contact with her clit and I twirl my finger around it once, twice, three times and then I feel it. Her walls flood with pleasure and I drive my cock into her harder. Her back arches and her mouth opens in a silent scream. She drops her head back and digs her nails into my back, my shoulders, my neck, wherever she can reach. The pleasure coursing through my veins only intensifies as the pain of her fingernails buzzes through me.

She gasps, inhaling loudly and tilting her head forward again to look at me. Her face is rapt. The moment I see the pure pleasure in her cloudy eyes I explode. I've never come like this before. I fill the condom again and again as she wraps her arms and legs around me. The pleasure explodes from my cock, sending electric shocks through every nerve ending in my body.

I collapse on top of her as I try to retain control over my ragged breath. My heart is hammering against my chest and I stay there. We hold each other until our bodies let us move again.

8

ROSIE

WHEN MY HEARTBEAT goes back down to normal, I open my eyes and trail my fingers over Lucas' back. He moans gently into my neck and lifts himself up to look at me, framing my face with his forearms.

"That was nice," he growls.

"Only nice?" I grin.

"Yeah," he says with a smirk. "It was okay."

I laugh and playfully smack his arm before running my fingers over his muscular shoulder and around his neck. He closes his eyes and sighs.

"Your touch is amazing."

"Your skin is amazing," I respond. We're like two love-struck teenagers instead of two full-grown adults who have just screwed each other's brains out. Is this what Jess had in mind when she said I needed to be royally Fucked with a capital 'F'? Somehow it seems like more than that. I wouldn't even call it casual sex, that cheapens what just happened.

Lucas dips his chin down and kisses my lips. I groan and wrap my arms around him until he pulls away.

"Where did you come from?" he breathes.

I grin. "I could ask you the same thing. If I remember correctly, it was *you* who barged in on *my* cab."

"Barged in!" His eyebrows shoot up. "You slithered your way in when I had my head turned for a second."

"*Slithered*," I repeat, painting exaggerated outrage on my face. "I'm a snake now, am I?"

"I knelt down to tie my shoelace and you pounced on the chance."

"That's not slithering my way in, that's capitalizing on an opportunity. And plus, the cab driver was clearly stopping for me."

"No way," Lucas shoots back, laughing. "He definitely saw me first."

"Agree to disagree," I say, shrugging and laughing as he lowers his face toward mine. He rubs his nose on mine, over and back, over and back, and then dips his lips down to meet mine. His kiss is soft and sweet, and I part my lips to taste him. I groan and sigh when he pulls away.

He sits up and looks down.

"Ahh, shit," he says under his breath. I look down to see the condom on the sofa. "Must have slid out just then."

"That's okay," I say as I sit up. "I'll grab a towel. The bathroom is just there."

Lucas nods and grabs the condom to throw it out. I get a rag from the kitchen and wipe the wet stain off the sofa. *Hopefully that doesn't leave a mark.*

I slip my panties back on and check the kitchen for something we can eat. My fridge is empty except for mustard and a block of cheese. I close it again and spot a bottle of wine in the cupboard. It's been there for months, Harper got it for me when I got out of the hospital. I usually just go for the cheapest bottle I can get but she actually knows good wine from bad. I grab the bottle and wipe off the dust.

"Perfect," I say to myself. I pop the cork and pour a couple glasses just as Lucas appears in the doorway, wearing his tight white boxers and undershirt. I hand him a glass of wine.

"Thanks," he says, never taking his eyes off me. "So what's a girl like you doing alone on her birthday?"

"I'm not alone," I reply with one eyebrow raised. I lift the glass to my lips and take a sip as I watch a grin play over his lips.

"Of all the cabs in all the streets in all of New York City, you walk into mine," he says with a sigh.

I lift a finger up. "*You* walk into *mine*, you mean."

His grin changes into a laugh that breaks his face open. His eyes shine as he laughs openly, with his mouth wide open. I like his laugh. I giggle as well and then we both take a drink.

"You're stubborn," he says. "I like that."

"Tenacious," I correct as I glance at him sideways and walk past him into the living room. I knock him gently with my hip on the way by and give him a wink.

"Right, tenacious. Persistent, even," he replies as he follows me. I sit down on the sofa, folding a leg underneath me and he takes a seat next to me. I glance at him over my wine glass as I take another sip.

"So where are you going tomorrow? Holiday?" I ask.

He shakes his head. "Back home to Los Angeles."

I nod and my mouth falls open. "Oh."

He smiles sadly and I look away. Did he look sad? I must be making things up. I take another drink and try to shake my thoughts away. This was a one-night thing, obviously. You don't pick someone up in a cab and expect to date them.

"I was in New York for business, been here ten days. I can't wait to go back, to be honest." He opens his mouth as if he's going to say something and then just lifts his wine glass and takes a drink. "This is nice stuff," he says as he lifts the glass toward me.

"Mm, yes," I say as I swirl my glass. "Tannins and… fruity notes. Dry tasting. Or whatever," I finish with a laugh. I shrug. "I don't really know anything about wine. It was a present."

He smiles. "Well, I'm glad you're sharing it with me. I'm flattered."

I glance at his face again and notice the little dimple in his left cheek. He smiles at me and desire stirs inside me again. The warmth in my core starts to blossom as I watch him take another sip.

It might be a one night thing, but at least I can enjoy it for the whole night. There are still a few hours for me to get royally Fucked again and again. And again.

9

LUCAS

ROSIE PUTS her glass down and comes closer to me on the sofa. I open my arms and she turns to lean back against my chest. I wrap my arm around her and trail my fingers across her clavicle. I feel her body relax into mine and my heartbeat slows. I lean back and close my eyes, but I know I won't sleep, not with this beautiful woman so close to me. My cock is already twitching as the warmth of her body rests over mine.

"What time is your flight?" she asks.

"8 am. I probably have to leave here around 5 at the latest. I haven't even packed yet."

"Who said you were sleeping over?" she says as she turns her head. I can see the corner of her lip curl upward and I chuckle.

"You wouldn't throw me out. You're too nice."

"You don't know that."

"I can tell," I say softly. It's true, I can. She has a warmth about her that's infectious. She makes me feel like I'm home.

Rosie turns around and drapes her arm over my chest. She pushes herself up so that our faces are just inches apart and she studies me for a few moments.

"I wasn't expecting my night to end like this," she says.

I pause. "Are you happy that it did?"

Her smile widens and her eyes sparkle that delicious green color. "I'm happy that it's not over yet."

She leans forward and crushes her lips against mine. Her kiss sends a jolt through my entire body, like an electric thrill coursing through my veins. She presses herself against me so that I can feel her breasts on my chest, her nipples hard as they rub against me. I wrap my fingers into her hair and kiss her harder.

Her body melts into mine and I know what bliss feels like. It's this. It's this woman in my arms, kissing me as if her life depended on it. It's the delicate perfume that she's wearing and the feel of her silky curls through my fingers. It's the heat of her body and the softness of her skin pressed against mine.

I want to enjoy every single minute that we have together. I wish I'd met her ten days ago, ten years ago! I wish I wasn't leaving in a few short hours and I could explore her body like I want to. I want to know everything about her, both body and mind. I want to make her grin and have her shoot that sideways look at me. I want to watch her laugh and see the way she tucks her hair behind her ear again.

I want to taste her. I want to bury my tongue inside her and suck her bud until she's grinding herself against my mouth and screaming my name. I want to drive my cock inside her deeper and harder than I did before, and then I want to sit back and watch her bounce on top of it.

I want it all. She writhes on top of me and moves to kiss my neck. She nibbles my earlobe and I chuckle, running my fingers down her spine to feel the curve of her ass. Her body is perfect, scars and all. She could do anything to me right now and my cock would feel like it's about to burst.

Rosie stands up in front of me and drops her panties. I

push my underwear down to my feet and kick them away. My cock springs forward and she grabs it in her hand. I groan as her fingers wrap themselves around my shaft. She strokes it once, twice, three times before lowering herself down.

I groan again when she rubs the tip of my cock back and forth over her slit. I can see her wetness on my cock, glistening in the low light of her apartment. I look up at her face and see her bite her lip as she closes her eyes.

She moans and my cock throbs in her hand. She rubs it back and forth and I know I won't be able to last much longer. The wetness of her slit against the tip of my cock is almost too much to bear. I want to come right now, like this.

"Condom," I breathe. "I need one now."

Her eyelids flutter open and her eyes are cloudy. It's like she's looking through me or inside me instead of at me. My cock throbs again and she nods. I look down at the floor and see my pants still bunched up there. I reach over to the pocket and am glad I always carry two condoms with me. I don't know why, it's not like I've used them in months, or longer.

I hardly have the condom rolled down my shaft when she's lowering herself on top of me. She lets out a long, low moan as she takes my full length inside her. I can feel her walls contract around my girth and I close my eyes and exhale.

"Fuck," I breathe.

She makes a noise halfway between pleasure and agreement, and then starts grinding her hips back and forth. She moves slowly, and I let my hands move up her thighs toward her hips. I sink my fingers into her ass cheeks and grind my hips into hers.

She opens her eyes and I see a spark in them. Her lips

curl upward the tiniest bit and she places a hand on my chest, bracing herself against me.

Then she starts.

Oh God, she starts.

It's like she read my mind. She bounces on my cock as I drive my hips up toward her. I gasp and groan as I watch her tits bounce up and down, using my hands to push her hips down on top of my cock harder and harder. The sound of our bodies colliding fills the room, loud slaps interspersed with grunts and groans and moans and yelps and screams and noises that make my head spin.

Her head falls backward and I watch her lips part, her hair bouncing with the rest of her body as she rides me like I've never been ridden before.

It's the feeling of her orgasm that sends me over the edge. Her whole body tenses and she grips my cock tighter than I thought possible. Her fingers dig into my chest and she slams herself down onto my cock. It feels like the breath leaves my body as I come, watching her beautiful pink lips make that soft 'o' and feeling her body spasm and contract.

She collapses on top of me and we lay motionless for an eternity. Slowly, I'm able to breathe again and open my eyes. After a few more minutes I'm able to think, and a few minutes after that I can speak.

"Wow," I say. She moans in response and all I can do is drop my lips down to kiss the top of her head. "Wow."

10

ROSIE

I WAKE up when he's disentangling himself from me to leave. I'm still mostly asleep when he places a soft kiss on my forehead.

"I'm leaving my number right here," he says. I groan in response, trying to open my eyes. "Don't get up. Call me later. If you want, obviously."

"I will," I say, finally opening my eyes. I sit up onto my elbows and watch as he pulls a shirt over his head. His abs move and stretch and the muscles in his arms ripple under his skin as he pulls the shirt down. He runs his fingers through his hair and looks at me, leaning over to kiss me again.

"I'm glad I met you," he says. I smile.

"Me too." I wish I could tell him how glad I am, or how sad I feel that he's leaving. I force a smile. "Now go, you'll miss your flight."

He nods and smiles, then turns and walks out. When I hear the front door click shut, I flop back down in bed and stare at the ceiling.

Wow.

My birthday definitely turned out better than expected. I turn toward my bedside table and pick up the scrap of paper with his number on it. I smile, bringing it up to my lips. He said he'd be back in New York, but he didn't know exactly when. He said to call him, that he wanted to come see me.

He said all these things and I feel like my heart is about to explode. I roll back over onto my back and sigh. My hand moves toward the scar on my ribs, a movement that has become a habit over the past six months. For the first time since it happened, the scars don't seem angry and ugly. He kissed them, touched them, made me feel like they were a beautiful part of me.

My fingers run up and down along the smooth line of skin and I remember the way his lips felt as they brushed against it. I've never felt so naked in front of anyone, or so comfortable. It's like he made me feel exposed and safe at the same time. I haven't felt at peace since the incident, and all at once he made me feel whole again.

I WAKE up a few hours later and roll over to the empty bed. I sigh. I wish I was waking up next to Lucas right now. I've never felt so strongly about someone after meeting them for just one night. I've never even had a one-night stand.

This doesn't feel like a one-night stand. How could it? It felt like there were two magnets pulling us together from the moment he sat down in that taxi.

I could text him right now, and let him know that I miss him already. I could tell him what a great time I had, and how glad I am that he barged in on my taxi.

But then again—would that be coming on too strong?

Maybe I should wait a couple hours. I could text him once he's in Los Angeles. I don't want to come across too eager. Maybe he was just saying those things in the moment, and once he lands he'll be back to his regular life and he'll forget all about me.

Somehow, I just can't bring myself to believe that's true. The way he looked at me, and the way he touched me and made me feel so alive—that has to be real.

I take a deep breath and smile. I'll text him in a few hours, that way he'll get it when he lands. Maybe Jess and Harper can help me write the message to get the right balance of enthusiasm and casualness.

My alarm starts buzzing on the night stand and I roll over to turn it off. I see a message from Jess.

Jess: Still on for brunch? Same spot?

I chuckle. She's not going to believe what's happened. I got a delayed birthday present that I was never expecting, and I scratched an itch that's been getting worse for months. I got royally Fucked with a capital F.

Rosie: Yeah, see you there. 10 am?

My phone buzzes a couple seconds later and I see a thumbs up from her. I look at the time—8:30. Perfect. Just enough time to shower and have some coffee at home. I can catch up on work emails that I missed yesterday and then head out to see the girls.

I thumb the scrap of paper and tuck it into the side pocket of my purse. I'll text him when I'm at brunch after I've filled Jess and Harper in on last night. I smile and stand up, stretching my arms above my head before doing a little dance from one foot to the other.

Even though I drank more than usual last night I don't feel hungover. It's like my night with Lucas just cleared all the cobwebs from my mind and set my body buzzing. He breathed new life into me and I can't help but smile and feel like it's the start of something new, something good. I finally feel like I'll be able to put the attack behind me and move on with my life.

11

LUCAS

TWELVE HOURS AGO, I couldn't wait to get back to LA to see my daughter. I was sick of New York and sick of the people and sick of the hustle and bustle of the city.

Now, I'm not so sure.

The final boarding call is announced and I check my phone for the hundredth time this morning. Still nothing from Rosie.

I sigh and tuck my phone away. She's probably still sleeping. We were up all night. I wish I'd asked her for her number before leaving, I'd have sent her a message telling her how much I enjoyed my time with her and how I couldn't wait to come back.

Now the ball is in her court, and I'll have to wait until she contacts me. It's fine, I'm sure she will. I just want her to do it quickly so I can tell her how much last night meant to me. The thought of leaving her now, after so little time, feels wrong.

I've never felt this kind of attraction to anyone before. Physical, mental, almost spiritual. The instant I saw her I knew that she was different. I knew she had to be mine. Ever since my wife died, I've felt like all I have left are work and Allie, but last night showed me something different. Maybe there's hope for me? Maybe there's a chance for me to be happy again?

I smile as I remember the way she pulled her foot away from me and almost sprinted down the street. I would have sat there, massaging her feet until the sun came up. I'd give anything to have her body in my arms right now.

My feet take me toward the gate and then down to the plane. My mind wanders as I put one foot in front of the other, waiting in the long line of people taking the same flight as me. I smile and nod as the flight attendants greet me as I get on, but my mind is all the way back at Rosie's apartment. I find my seat and sit down and can't resist the temptation any longer. I pull out my phone and my heart drops as I see the blank screen. I have a photo of Allie and me as my background, and I click the side of my phone to make it go back to sleep.

She hasn't texted me, but it isn't even 8 am yet. We were up all night on top of each other. She's probably still asleep, and I need to relax. What I feel right now is real, it has to be. I know she felt it too. I'll just go back to LA, start talking to her and see how it goes. At the end of the day, my life is on the West coast and I have a daughter to take care of. I can't let one night get in the way of my whole life.

I need to remind myself of the important things right now. I'm going back to my daughter and I have a massive workload for the next few weeks until this launch is out of the way. Maybe it's good that I'm leaving New York, because I know that Rosie would be a distraction.

I purse my lips as the thought crosses my mind. I can't call her a distraction, it's wrong. She is anything but a distraction. She's beautiful and funny and smart and witty and she's got that sarcastic bite that I love. She's not a distraction, it would be a privilege to have her in my life.

I wake up my phone one last time and sigh. The air hostess comes down the aisle and sees it in my hand.

"Hi sir, please turn your phone off for takeoff. Thank you." She turns to the row behind me and asks them to move their seats up.

I purse my lips but flick my phone on airplane mode. Surely by the time I land she'll have messaged me.

12

ROSIE

"You did *what*?" Jess's jaw is on the floor and Harper is staring at me like I have three heads. Her fork is hanging in the air halfway between her plate and her mouth.

"I can't explain it, it's like we were just drawn to each other."

"You little hussy," Jess says with a grin. "I didn't think you had it in you."

"I had *it* in me last night, that's for sure," I respond with a laugh. Jess bursts out laughing and smacks the table with her hand.

"Rosie Michelle Jackson, I have never been prouder of you than I am right now."

I grin. "I've never been this proud of myself either, if I'm honest. I need your help though."

"What do you need?" Harper asks right away. She's always been the most loyal and loving friend. Helping is an instinct to her. I laugh.

"Nothing difficult. I need help writing my message to him. I want him to know how great last night was but I don't want to come on too strong."

"Definitely," Jess replies. Harper nods once with a knowing look on her face.

"Yeah, these next few days will be crucial."

"So what do I say? Like... Thanks for screwing my brains out last night? It was fun?"

"Yes. Tell him how beautiful his cock was," Jess replies with a laugh. She turns toward me and holds up her hands as if she just thought of something. "He did have a beautiful cock, right? I mean, if we're putting effort into making this guy come back across the country it better be worth it."

I shake my head. "He has the most beautiful cock I've ever seen. And the things he did with his hands, with his tongue..." my voice trails off and I stare into the black coffee in my mug, feeling the memories of my orgasms last night.

"What did he do?" Harper asks almost breathlessly. I glance up at her, remembering the both of them are here.

"I can't describe it. He was just.... He was good. He was really good."

Jess laughs and claps her hands. "Okay, get your phone out. Let's write this message."

I smile and pull out my phone, grateful to have such supportive friends. Jess has started composing already.

"So you want to sound enthusiastic but not overly eager. Start with 'Hey,'," she pauses, taking a bite of pancake and chewing thoughtfully. "'Hey, hope you had a good flight.' Then put some emoji, maybe a smiley face."

I nod, tapping a blank message on my phone. Jess continues.

"'Hey, hope you had a good flight, smiley face, I had a great time last night. Winky face.'"

Harper pipes up. "No, delete the first smiley, one emoji is enough. You don't want to come across as juvenile."

I laugh and tap some more on my phone. The three of us go back and forth until I've written the perfect message.

Rosie: Hey, I had an amazing time last night 😜 *Hope you had a smooth flight!*

I glance at the girls and my eyebrows shoot up as I inhale. "This is it."

Jess claps her hands and Harper laughs. "Do it!"

"Just have to get his number. I have it here," I say, grabbing my purse. I rifle through the pocket looking for the scrap of paper. I frown when I can't find it in the pocket I thought I put it in. I look in another pocket, and then in the main compartment. I pause and glance at my friends.

Jess's lips stretch out into an awkward cringe. "Can't find it?"

"It's here, I know it is. It must have fallen into the main pocket." I start pulling things out of my purse and sigh with every new item. Four Chapsticks, two lipsticks, wallet, charger, mini deodorant, spare undies, tampons, old gum wrappers, three pens.

All the junk in my purse is on the table and I turn the lining inside out. My heart feels like a stone sinking down to my stomach.

"It's not here. I know I put it in here. I have literal garbage in my purse and I don't have his fucking number!"

"Don't panic," Harper says as she reaches over to put her hand on my forearm. "Maybe you took it out, maybe it's at home or on the ground in your room or something."

I take a deep breath and nod. "Yeah, you're right. No sense panicking until I've checked everywhere." I smile with tight lips and start putting things back in my purse. I can't help the feeling of dread growing in my stomach. I know I put his number in here. I remember putting it in here, so where is it?

I check the ground around me and can't shake the feeling that I've lost it.

Why didn't I just save his number right away? Who even writes their number on paper anymore?

I put my purse down and stare at the plate of food in front of me. I've hardly eaten half of it but my appetite has disappeared. Jess and Harper exchange a glance and then look at me. Jess speaks first.

"Don't panic, Rosie. You'll find it. And if not, we can put our expert FBI-level social media stalking skills to use. We'll find him."

I nod and try to relax my shoulders down. "You're right," I say as I take a bite of hash brown. "This is the twenty-first century. I'll find him." I smile again, this time a bit more easily. "Thanks."

Jess shrugs. "What can I say, I'm a hopeless romantic."

Harper snorts and the three of us laugh. I glance at my friends and feel a wave of love for them. I don't know where I'd be without them.

13

LUCAS

THE PILOT ANNOUNCES the start of the descent and my heart jumps. Surely Rosie will have contacted me by now.

That thought has carried me through the last six and a half hours. I've replayed our night from start to finish, trying to anchor the memory in my head before it fades. I can picture her body as if she was right in front of me, tracing the scars on her body in my mind's eye. I can see her smile. I can smell her hair. When I close my eyes it's almost as if she's there, but then I open them again and she's gone.

It's bizarre, this feeling. It's bizarre to have such a strong connection with someone after hardly knowing them. I just hope she's texted me.

As soon as the wheels touch down in Los Angeles my phone is in my hand again and I've flicked off airplane mode. My heart beats a little bit faster as it connects to the network and starts buzzing with emails and messages. I click on the notifications excitedly and scan the list for a new number.

My heart sinks as the notifications come to a stop and I realize she hasn't sent me anything. I open the messages that have come though one by one and close them again.

Allie sent me a message. I still can't believe she can use her phone better than I can.

Allie: *Welcome home Dad! Can't wait to see you!*

I smile despite myself.

Lucas: *Just landed kiddo. See you soon.*

I slip my phone into my pocket and stand up as the plane starts to disembark. I feel my phone vibrate in my pocket and my heart jumps. It's probably Allie, but I can't help but wonder if Rosie has sent me anything.

Shaking my head, I try to push the thought away. I'm being ridiculous. I'm a grown man. I've known her for *one night*. For all I know she could never call me again. It was probably just a one-night stand for her, and here I am fantasizing about seeing her again.

My mind pushes and pulls back and forth as I get off the plane and get my luggage. It's not until I'm out of the taxi and opening the front door of my house that the thoughts dissipate. Allie comes running full speed and jumps into my arms as soon as I step inside.

"Daddy!"

"Hey, kiddo," I say as I wrap my arms around her and spin her in a circle in the foyer. I put her back down and she jumps up excitedly.

"I missed you! How was New York? Come see your surprise!"

I laugh and ruffle her hair. She ducks her head away and sticks her bottom lip out in an exaggerated pout.

"My hair!"

"It still looks beautiful kid."

"Don't call me kiddo anymore, dad, I'm going to be twelve next month."

"You're right. What should I call you? Young lady?"

She rolls her eyes and I stifle a grin. "Call me Allie, Dad. It's my name, remember?"

"Hi, Lucas," my mother's voice comes down the hallway. "How was the flight, honey?"

"It was fine, Mom. Thanks again for watching Allie. I know it was way longer than expected, I'll make it up to you, I promise."

"It was no bother at all," my mom says as she plants a kiss on my cheek. "Allie and I had a great time. I love the company. Ever since your father died, I'm on my own a lot. It's nice to spend some time with my favorite granddaughter."

"Still," I say, as I ruffle my daughter's hair again. She squeals and jumps back, patting her hair down.

I laugh and carry my suitcase inside. Allie grabs my carry-on bag and helps me bring it up to my room. As soon as the bags are down, she slips her hand into mine and brings me to the kitchen.

"Grandma and I made cookies for you! Chocolate chip peanut butter, your favorite."

"Yum!"

We make our way to the kitchen and Allie fills me in on the past week and a half. I try to keep up and can't resist taking a look at my phone. Allie puts her hands on her hips and takes a step back. "Why are you looking at your phone? You look different."

"Different? I'm just tired, kid—Allie. Long flight."

"No, not tired. Different. Your eyes are shiny. What happened?"

I shake my head and put my phone back in my pocket. "Nothing happened, kiddo."

"Allie," she corrects. I grin.

"Allie. Nothing happened. I'm glad to be back. Where's my surprise?"

Allie's eyes narrow and she takes a step toward me, craning her face toward mine. She studies me for a few seconds and I do my best to look casual. My phone is burning a hole in my pocket, conspicuous in its complete silence. Still nothing from Rosie.

My daughter takes a deep breath and nods her head. "Okay. You're normal."

My mother laughs and I see her shake her head. "That daughter of yours is something else," she says with a smile.

"She's like her grandmother. Aren't you, Allie?"

"I'm like *myself*."

I laugh and my mother squeezes my shoulder. Allie beckons me toward the living room and presents me with an elaborate drawing of her, me, and my mom.

"It's our family."

I smile and my heart finally feels calm. I'm home. "It's amazing, Allie. Did you draw this yourself? We'll have to frame it and hang it up."

Allie is beaming. I slip my phone out of my pocket and put it on the counter. Whether Rosie texts or not doesn't seem so important right now. Now I need to spend time with my daughter.

14

ROSIE

I FLOP down onto my bed and stare at the floor. I can't find it anywhere. I've lost it. My heart sinks like a stone and Jess comes over to sit beside me.

"We'll find him on Facebook. What did you say his job was?"

"I don't know."

"What's his last name?"

"I don't know."

"Where does he live? Do you know any specifics besides Los Angeles?"

"I don't know," I snap. "I don't know anything about him. I know his name is Lucas and he lives in Los Angeles. I know he likes wine."

I sigh. I rack my memory, trying to think of other things. We talked about everything and nothing, about life and happiness and sex but somehow, I don't seem to know a single thing about him. Jess puts her hand on my thigh.

"We'll find him," she says gently. "Don't worry."

I look over at her and smile. Her dark brown hair is pulled up into a messy bun and she pushes her dark-rimmed glasses up her nose. She smiles at me and nods. "We'll find him."

"Okay," I respond with a sigh. "You're right. No use getting all upset. It's just... why didn't I save his number right away? I always lose things! The one time I meet someone I actually like. The first time in months I feel comfortable around a man."

"Don't beat yourself up about it, Rosie. It happens all the time to everyone. And it was only a scrap of paper. I'd be more surprised if you *hadn't* lost it."

I smile. I know she's only trying to make me feel better but it's working despite my best efforts to be grumpy.

"Come on," Jess says as she gets up off my bed. "Let's go do something to make us feel better. We'll get a pedicure and we can start our Facebook stalking while we're there. By the end of it all you'll have sent him a text and you'll have pretty toes. Win-win."

"That sounds nice."

The two of us get up and Jess gives me a hug. I'm so mad at myself, but I try to forget it as we head to our favorite nail salon. I'm starting to feel hopeful as we sit down and start getting our feet scrubbed and clipped and painted. Jess makes me laugh as we start looking online, searching every possible combination and looking through profile after profile.

My heart starts to sink as Jess shows me yet another Lucas from Los Angeles that isn't *my* Lucas from Los Angeles. I shake my head and Jess purses her lips.

"Let's widen our search. We don't even know if this guy is on Facebook. He could be one of those private people. Which," she glances at me. "Red flag, am I right?" I roll my eyes and laugh. Jess continues: "How about LinkedIn? You said he had files and a bag? He talked about work? Surely, he's got LinkedIn. Even old people in the workforce have LinkedIn. My uncle Bert has LinkedIn."

I nod, but it's starting to feel hopeless. We've been looking for him online for over an hour. Jess can find anybody within minutes if you give her their hair color and their cousin's brother's name. She's a wizard at looking for people on social media and she's coming up empty.

"I'm starting to wonder if he even exists at all," I say as I start scrolling through profile after profile. "Maybe it was all a dream."

"Maybe," Jess says absent-mindedly. "It wasn't him was it?"

She turns her phone toward me and I see an overweight old man who's got to be at least 70. He's holding a rubber chicken in one hand and a beer in the other. I laugh.

"No, not him."

"Shame. I was going to high-five you. Might send old Lucas Miller here a message." She shakes her head. "Imagine having that as your LinkedIn profile picture. Has this guy ever had a job?"

"Maybe in 1929," I respond with a grin.

Jess laughs and nods at my toes. "Looking good. I love that color."

I glance down at the bright coral pink on my toes. "Thanks. Thought I'd branch out a bit. New year, new me kind of thing."

"Post orgasm pedicure," she responds.

I can't help but laugh. Even though we haven't found Lucas, I'm glad I have a good friend here next to me. She reaches over and puts her hand on my forearm.

"We'll find him," she says gently, as if she read my mind. My throat starts to close up and I struggle to swallow. I can only nod my head and she winks at me before turning to her own toes. She's chosen a jet black color and she wiggles them proudly.

"Dark, just like my soul," she says.

I laugh and shake my head. "Far from it, Jess. You're a sweetheart."

"A sweetheart with goth toes," she replies. "Let's get a manicure as well. I need a break from all that Googling. It's hard work. I can have goth fingers as well, and then no one will know I have a heart."

I laugh and nod my head. "Fine," I reply with a smile. She winks at me and once again I'm grateful to have her.

15

LUCAS

As the days went by, I stopped checking my phone. The days turned into weeks and her silence went from a deafening roar to a dull ache inside me, and now a distant memory. I didn't know that I could care so much about a woman I knew for only a few hours, but the connection we had was different.

At least, I *thought* it was. It was different for me, but obviously it wasn't for her. She said she hadn't been with a man in months and she played the part of a nervous, innocent young woman very well. It was obviously all an act. My bitterness has faded now, or at least it's dulled a bit.

Life went on. Allie is doing well at school, the launch was successful, I've been promoted at work. I'm now the managing agent for seventeen of the top twenty singers currently on the pop charts. Maybe if I prove myself I'll be able to get the Assistant Director's position. I've already told my boss, Linda, that I'm sick of all the travel. Life is good, or at least it should be.

I haven't thought of Rosie in a while, until I'm walking down Melrose Avenue and I see a woman walking in front of me with the same curly red hair, the same tall, willowy figure. My heart skips a beat. Why would she be in Los Angeles? Surely, it's not her. I find myself speeding up, trying to catch up to her. My feet take me closer and closer and her name is on my lips. I open my mouth, ready to call out to her just as she turns around.

My heart jumps and I reach out, the smile already breaking across my face. Her head turns and all my hopes fall away.

It's not her. Our eyes meet for an instant and I see her frowning slightly. I look away, trying to shuffle past her without her noticing my disappointment. The woman is beautiful and young, maybe an aspiring actress, but she's not Rosie. My heart drops and I shake my head, sighing loudly.

Of course it isn't her. What would she be doing here? Wandering the streets of Los Angeles hoping to run into me? And even if it was her, why should I be happy? I should be mad at her, upset that she ignored me. Her silence should say it all—she doesn't want anything to do with me.

What would I even say to her? Would I try to be cordial, to have polite conversation? Should I get mad at her and let her know that I waited for her to call for days, no, *weeks*?

I feel like an idiot.

I stomp down the street without looking back at the woman that isn't Rosie. I don't want to see another red-haired woman again. They've lost their appeal to me.

Truthfully, all women have. I don't go out, I don't notice the appeal to any of the glamorous, rich, successful artists that I manage. I don't see any of it. It feels exactly like when my wife died. Life seems just a little bit more pointless, a little bit more empty.

I knew this woman for *one night*. Get a fucking grip.

I'm just stressed. It's work, I tell myself. I'm just focusing on Allie, and on work. Those are the important things, not a one night stand I had when I was on a business trip.

Still, sometimes I find my thoughts drifting back to that night. The way her body tasted, the way she looked in the dim light, the way her laugh would ring out and I couldn't help but smile. I had so many questions for her. Where was she from? What did she do? How did she get those scars? What was her favorite food? Favorite music? Favorite movie?

One night. That's all I had. I didn't ask any of it, but I still feel like I know her.

After that night my whole mindset changed. I don't see anything except Allie, and work. Work and Allie. Allie and work. It's better this way. I can focus. There aren't any distractions.

I hail a cab and smile as I sit down, thinking of the way we met. I tell the cab driver the address of my office and he grunts in response before stepping on the gas. I push the thought out of my mind and sigh. Rosie is gone, and I have to put her out of my mind for good.

The moment I step out of the elevator and into our offices, I'm hit with a barrage of voices.

"Lucas. Lucas! Did you hear?"

"Hey, Jake, what's up?" I ask, shuffling my bag off and dropping it on a table.

"McKinley and Lee, they've closed down." My heart stops for the second time today. All the blood drains from my face and I turn to my second-in-command.

"What?"

"They've closed down. It's shocked us all. They just shut their doors and liquidated their business. We've been trying to get Max on the phone but it's disconnected. They're saying he left the country."

My hand flies up to my forehead and I run my fingers

through my hair. I blow all the air out of my lungs and look at Jake, shaking my head.

"What?"

It's all I can manage to say. He lifts his shoulders up and lets them drop back down. "What are we going to do? We have seventeen active campaigns."

This is disastrous. We'll drop off the charts and lose millions if we can't keep pushing the artists' advertising campaigns. Max's agency was the biggest on the East coast, and now it's just *gone*??

"I've compiled a list of alternative agencies," Jake responds, producing a paper. "The one at the top would be my choice. They got a new CEO," he glances at the paper, "Uh, Zach Lockwood, he took over a few years ago. He's turned it around and now they're giving McKinley and Lee a run for their money. They'll be the new big hitter in the market."

I grab the paper and scan the names. All the other agencies are second-rate, at best.

"Get me a flight. And get me Lockwood on the phone!" I call out, heading toward my office. "I'm going to New York."

I close the door to my office and slump down on my chair. My head is spinning. Maybe Rosie wasn't in Los Angeles this morning but I'll sure as hell be in New York by tomorrow.

16

ROSIE

Two little blue lines. The second one is faint, but it's there. I'm still sitting on the toilet, pants around my ankles, staring at those two little blue lines. The harder I stare the darker they seem to get, taunting me.

I bring a hand to my stomach and look down. I knew something was wrong, but *pregnant*? Me?

The only time I've had sex was with Lucas. And we used protection! Sure, the condom slipped off the first time after we were done and I wasn't exactly careful the second time before we started but surely that can't lead to pregnancy? Maybe it was defective.

I stare at the two little blue lines again. They're still there, still taunting me.

I'm pulled out of my thoughts when someone barges into the work bathroom. It's Harper.

"Rosie," she calls out, breathless. "Rosie!"

"In here," I say, putting the pregnancy test on top of the toilet roll holder and pulling up my pants. "One sec."

"Rosie, since McKinley and Lee have closed down, we're

getting calls left right and center. Do you still have those drafts of the campaigns you showed me a few weeks ago?"

I frown. "The ones I did because I thought their campaigns were garbage? For the pop stars?"

"Yes! Get this: we've just gotten a call from the managing agent for *seventeen* of the top twenty charting artists. They want to move their whole portfolio over."

I open the stall door, frowning. "There's no way we can handle that kind of workload."

"If you still have all that work done, we can! You basically created full draft campaigns for multiple artists. Rosie, Zach said if they're good, he'll put you in charge of the whole portfolio!"

My head is spinning. I see Harper's eyes flick to the top of the toilet roll holder and then back to me. Her eyes widen until I can see the whites all around her irises.

"Rosie..." she breathes.

I grab the pregnancy test and hold it up for her to see. "My birthday," I explain. She takes it in her hand and stares at the two little blue lines, just like I did.

"Sometimes the tests are defective," she says, shaking her head. "Take another one tomorrow."

"It's the fourth one I've taken. I've already spent almost $50. Harper, I'm pregnant."

Harper's mouth hangs open. She shakes her head.

"No, Rosie, that's not supposed to happen." She looks at me, mouth agape. "I'm the one who had a surprise pregnancy, not you! You're the smart one."

"We used protection. I don't know what happened."

I take the test back and stare at it again. I walk to the garbage can and toss it away. I turn back to Harper.

"I've got like seven months to figure that out. When is this agent coming? At least if I have a shitload of work to focus on,

64

I won't panic." I pause. Harper's face is drawn with concern. "...Yet. I won't panic yet."

A smile breaks on her face and she extends her arms. I walk toward her and she hugs me tightly, cooing and whispering in my ear.

"It'll be okay," she says. "I'm here, and I've been through it all. It'll be okay."

It's hard to believe her but it's still comforting to hear the words. She squeezes me a bit tighter and then pulls away, putting her hands on my upper arms. She gives them a squeeze and looks at me with tears in her eyes.

"This probably isn't what you want to hear, but having Mary was the best thing that ever happened to me. I never wanted kids and now I'm happier than I've ever been."

I smile sadly. Harper is married to the CEO, Zach Lockwood. She's had a baby and a wedding and met her soulmate. Somehow being a single mother struggling on one salary doesn't really seem like the same thing, but I hold my tongue. All I can do is force a smile and nod. I blink back the tears in my eyes and try to ignore the prickling in my eyelids.

Harper hugs me again and I let a tear fall down before pulling away and turning to the mirror to fix my makeup.

"Okay, so what are the artists?" I say a little bit louder. "I have draft campaigns for six of them but they can be adjusted pretty easily. I think hitting social media harder than McKinley and Lee were is going to be more effective. We need to go where the customers are."

"Definitely. Don't tell me, tell the agent. He's landing in New York tonight and wants a meeting first thing tomorrow morning. Can you have a deck ready for 7 am? Just two of your best campaigns, updated for current singles and albums." Harper opens the bathroom door and we step out. "We'll want to make the transition to our campaign as seamless as possible, so you'll have to explain how that will work, and how we'll scale up the social media and scale down the traditional advertising."

"Right." I pause. "Harper, I've never done this before. You know, lead something this big."

Harper stops and turns toward me, smiling. "You're talented and confident and hard-working. Zach wouldn't give this to you if he didn't think you could do it. If *I* didn't think you could do it. You've already done all the work and now you just need to show it off. And like you said, it'll get your mind off the other thing."

I nod and take a deep breath. The strength inside me grows a little and I stand up straighter.

"You're right. Okay, I'll have it ready for 7 am."

"I called a sitter so I'll stay as long as you need me tonight. We have the rest of the team working on the financials and the bones of the proposal, but we need your content and your creative direction.

I nod again and start walking to my desk. The pregnancy test is gone for now at the bottom of the garbage can. Between now and tomorrow morning I won't think of the baby growing inside me. I won't think of Lucas, or single motherhood, or diapers or cribs or anything except delivering this advertising campaign as well as I can.

Harper's right, this is a blessing in disguise. I get to my desk and glance up to see Harper looking at me from across the room. She smiles slightly and dips her chin down. I nod as well and can't help but smile back. This is what I'm good at.

17

LUCAS

THE WHEELS TOUCH DOWN and my heart jumps. I try to ignore the image in my head—the image of Rosie in front of me with her head back as I kiss her body from head to toe. I've seen it in my mind's eye almost every day for the past two months.

I'm back.

I know I won't see her—New York is a city of eight and a half million people. It was already blind luck to run into her once, it won't happen again.

Besides, it's better this way. What would I even say to her? Show up at her house and just say: *Got the message, you want nothing to do with me.* Or maybe pretend like nothing happened. *Hey, what's up?*

There's no point thinking like this. I won't see her, so it's a waste of time anyway.

I have bigger things to worry about. My clients' success and future hangs in the balance and is completely dependent on the deals I can negotiate with Lockwood's firm. They must know that I need them. They'll be able to charge me whatever they want and I'll have to accept. All I can do is use the fame of my clients and bluff my way through these meetings.

I make my way off the plane and I feel no less nervous than I did when I left LA. The next few days are critical not only for my clients but for my own career. I'm thinking about Rosie, and worried about what hypothetical me would say when I hypothetically run into her when the bigger problem is what I'll actually say when I'm locked in negotiations for the next three days.

I sling my small carry-on bag over my shoulder and make my way toward the exit. I don't expect I'll be in New York for more than three or four days and I've packed light.

6:01 am. I should be at the firm's offices by 7 am, just in time for my first meeting. They assured me they'd have a proposal ready but I don't know what they could have done in such a short amount of time. I'm not expecting much.

I jump in a cab and give the driver the address. Staring out the window, I remember driving in the opposite direction. I remember how happy I was when I left Rosie, how hopeful I'd been about pursuing this crazy connection I thought we had.

Now it's just bitterness. The thought of her makes the anger curl up my spine and close around my throat like a black hand. The thought of my rejection, of the hours I spent wishing she would call.

It's embarrassing.

I was a one night stand for her, and like a fool I thought it meant more. I'm not usually like this, and I don't know why it was different with her. *Was* it even different with her? Maybe it wasn't, but I've been so focused on work, so focused on Allie that I've forgotten what it's like to be with a woman.

Maybe it wasn't different at all.

Maybe it wasn't special, it wasn't a connection, it didn't mean anything.

I mean, she never called, so of course it didn't mean anything. She made me feel like it did, and then she just disappeared.

A part of me knows I can't blame her. We met, we had sex, and then I left to go back home on the other side of the country. What kind of relationship is that? What kind of future would there be?

I shake my head and sigh. I'm finding excuses to avoid the relationship that I never even had in the first place. These thoughts are pointless. She didn't want me, and she didn't call. We had one good night and that's it. I should be grateful I got laid that night at all.

Still, when I close my eyes and try to focus on the meetings I'm heading to, all I see is the little freckle on her cheek and the way she tucked her hair behind her ear. How can I have such a clear image of her after two months? We only spent a few hours together!

The cab driver stops in front of a tall office building and clicks a button on the meter.

"$42.25," he says unceremoniously.

I sigh and hand him fifty dollars. "Keep the change."

Stepping out of the cab, I stare up at the wall of windows in front of me. There must be fifty or sixty floors in this building. I straighten my tie and take a breath, walking through the revolving glass doors and heading to the wall to look for Lockwood Advertising. I scan the list of businesses and find the name with 'Level 43' next to it.

With one last breath, Rosie disappears from my mind and I put my game face on. It's time to negotiate like my life depends on it and make sure I can secure my clients' futures. Some chick I slept with a few months ago shouldn't even register in my mind right now. I have way more important things to take care of.

The elevator doors close as I press the little round button with number 43 on it. It lights up and I take a step back, squaring my shoulders and inhaling deeply as I feel the elevator whizz upward.

A familiar sense of calm comes over me and I know I'm in the zone. Nothing can throw me off now. I know what I need to negotiate and I know what I can offer. I should be in and out in a couple hours and then I can go back to Los Angeles and forget about Rosie once and for all.

18

ROSIE

IT'S 6:52 AM, which means the agent will be here any minute. I smooth down the front of my skirt and skim my fingers over the scar on my ribs. My hand trails over my stomach for a second before I let it drop. I wonder how many more scars and stretch marks I'll have on my abdomen when this baby is born?

The thought doesn't scare me, it excites me. Somehow the thought of my body changing to create another human fills me with the deepest sense of wonder and excitement I've ever felt. I square my shoulders and stack the notes for my proposal before heading to the conference room. Every decision now feels more important, like the fate of my baby rests entirely on my shoulders. This proposal, my career, my health—it all means so much more than it did before.

I get to the conference room and put my hands on my hips as I look around the room. The projector is set up, my laptop has the proposal deck queued and I have my notes ready.

This is the biggest project I've ever led, and definitely the most responsibility I've ever had. This client is critical. If we land this contract, it'll add a good 30% more business to our portfolio and put us as the #1 advertising firm on the East coast. The pressure is immense.

I just hope it's good enough.

Harper has told me time and again that I'm talented, that I have a good eye, that I know what sells, but there's always a voice at the back of my mind that says it's not enough. It's not modern enough, it's not on trend enough, it's not sharp enough.

If this proposal isn't enough, the loss will be on my shoulders. I glance at my notes and sigh. These are all mockups that I did in my spare time, basically just to prove that McKinley & Lee didn't deserve to be the top advertising firm in the city. They're not exactly polished.

I try to shake the thought out of my head and take a cleansing breath. I know this agent needs us and that his clients need us. He's just been dropped in the middle of God-knows-how-many advertising campaigns. He needs a new advertising contract immediately, and we can deliver it.

But still, as much as he needs us, I need him to buy into my proposal. We need him just as much as he needs us, but we can't let it show.

I glance at the clock. 6:57 am. The minutes are crawling by.

Harper slips into the conference room and gives me an encouraging smile.

"You'll be great. You got this."

"I don't know Harps, a lot of it is just sloppy. I was mostly just messing around when I made these."

"Rosie, they're good. You're talented and this is way more than any other firm will have. You got this. Zach wouldn't have chosen you as lead if he didn't think you could do it."

I nod just as Zach walks in. He squeezes Harper's

shoulder as he walks by her and I feel a pang in my chest. They found each other last year and within a couple months were madly in love with a baby on the way.

My hand drifts to my stomach again and I feel the familiar loneliness start to curdle inside me.

"I need a coffee," I announce, trying to ignore the feeling. "Anyone else?"

"Sure," Harper says as Zach shakes his head. I nod and head out toward the office kitchen.

My hands are shaking as I grab two mugs. I'm not even supposed to be drinking coffee, but I have to make an exception this morning. It'll calm my nerves and give me something to do before he gets here.

The coffee is dark and strong, steam curling up from the mugs as I pick them up and head back to the conference room. I can hear voices inside. Harper, Zach, and a man's voice. I frown as something inside me recognizes the voice. Where have I heard it before?

Instinctively, I know where I've heard it before, but it can't be him. My mind must be playing tricks on me. It's not him, it must be the nerves.

I take a deep breath and turn the corner toward the door. Just two more steps and I'll be there, about to have the biggest moment of my career thus far. I step through the doorway and immediately freeze as my eyes lock onto the agent who's here to hear my proposal. My jaw drops and I let the two mugs fall down a couple inches. The coffee splashes up the sides but doesn't spill on the ground.

My mouth is suddenly dry and I close it again, licking my lips to try to speak. Finally my vocal cords start working and I say the name that's been on my mind for the past three months.

"Lucas?" It comes out as a squeak.

He's here. He's sitting across from Zach, dressed in a white shirt and navy suit. His hair is styled and he looks just as attractive as the last time I saw him, maybe even more. The nervousness inside me blossoms into desire as I see the man that I've been missing. Time slows down as he turns his head toward me, his clear blue eyes lifting to meet mine.

The father of my child.

He's just as shocked as I am, but recovers more quickly. He closes his mouth and his eyes harden. His stare is cold and he dips his chin down once.

"Rosie."

His coldness pierces through me like a dagger. He looks down at the paperwork in front of him and I glance at Harper. My eyes widen and I feel my mouth open and close like a goldfish. Suddenly I'm off balance.

Harper clears her throat. "You two know each other?" Her voice is steady but her eyes are questioning me.

Lucas answers before I can.

"We met once," he says shortly. "Should we get started?"

"Of course," Zach jumps in, giving me a meaningful stare.

I'm still speechless. I nod and put a mug of coffee down next to Harper. She squeezes my forearm and looks at me again with a face full of questions. I glance away, trying to ignore the thumping in my chest.

The world has tilted sideways and I'm scrambling to keep my footing. I walk around the table toward my computer and stare at the screen. I can't make out any of the words. I can't remember any of the proposal. I can't even remember what this is about. I'm completely blank.

The most important moment of my career has just turned into the most uncomfortable moment of my personal life, and I'm not sure how I'll make it through the next hour without bursting into tears or screaming at the top of my lungs.

"Whenever you're ready," Harper says softly. I glance at her and she nods. Her stare fills me with strength and I take a deep breath. The letters on the screen rearrange themselves into words and I remember why I'm here.

"Right. Let's get started."

19

LUCAS

I DON'T HEAR the first twenty minutes of her proposal. My mind is running circles around me as I try to understand what's going on.

I mean, I know what's going on. She's the editor in charge of my proposals. That's clear. What I can't figure out is how I came to be sitting at this table without realizing she would be here.

God, she looks good. That skirt is hugging her curves perfectly, and her hair is pinned back to show her graceful slender neck. She's standing sideways and all I want to do is kiss that little spot just below her ear.

Just as the thought crosses my mind, I push it away. This is the woman who ignored me, who left me hanging and had me believe there might be something more. Sure it was one night, and everything inside me told me to forget about her, but for some reason the rejection stung more than usual.

It's a constant tug-of-war in my mind. On the one hand, she looks amazing and all I want to do is talk to her and convince her to go out with me again, for real this time. On the other hand, she made herself very clear when she never bothered to tell me she wasn't interested. The least she could have done was texted me to tell me, but even that was too much effort.

".. and we forecast that this combined with the social media campaign will give you at least a 150% return."

Rosie turns to face me and I realize that I haven't heard a word of what she's said. I clear my throat and glance down at the printout that they've given me. Her work is good, there's no denying that. Maybe even better than the last advertising firm. But how can I consider hiring them? I'd have to see her and talk to her all the time.

I nod and glance at Zach Lockwood. I can't look at her, so he's the next best thing. His face is unreadable. "This looks very good. Would you be able to give me a few days to review everything and consult with the artists?"

"Of course. Can we expect an answer by the end of the week? As you can appreciate, it'll take some time to launch the campaign."

"I'll have an answer by close of business tomorrow."

"Great," he says, and stands up to shake my hand. The commercial director, Harper, stands and does the same. They leave the office and before I know it, I'm alone with Rosie. She's tidying her papers and stands up when I do.

Finally, our eyes meet again. I haven't looked at her since she walked in the door and almost knocked me off my chair.

"Lucas," she starts. Her hand brushes her ribs and I remember the scars that marked her body. I feel an almost magnetic pull toward her and all I want to do is take her in my arms, but then I remember she doesn't want me. This is an act. Her eyes are almost pleading and I tighten my lips into a thin line. I don't want to hear her excuses, to hear her apologize for ignoring me or whatever she's about to tell me. I don't even want to hear her voice. It sounds too nice and makes my resolve weaken. I interrupt her.

"Thanks for all that work, Rosie. You're clearly talented. Like I said before I'll have an answer by the end of business tomorrow. I just need to speak with my clients."

She looks surprised, her eyebrows jump up a fraction of an inch but she nods quickly, rearranging her face with a mask of professionalism. She glances down at her things and closes her laptop gently, unplugging it from the projector.

"Of course, thank you for coming in this morning. Let me know if you have any questions about the mockups."

"Will do."

I brush past her, making sure not to touch her body. I keep my head down and stalk out of the room. It's not until I'm in the elevator on the way down that I realize I've been holding my breath. I let it all out at once and all of a sudden feel like I'm about to fall over. The elevator doors open and I stumble out, making my way to the street and into a cab toward my hotel.

Somehow, I'm able to keep it together until I get into my hotel room and collapse on the bed. My hands fly up to my face and I groan as I rub my eyes.

I turn over and grab the stack of papers that I got at Rosie's office. Her proposal is good. Excellent, even. I'd be a fool to turn it down. I thumb through the papers and shake my head. Even the artists will be able to tell this is smarter and sharper than the last campaign launch. They're waiting on my call, so it's not like I can pretend I don't have it.

I have two more meetings with other firms today but I already know this will be the best. Unless I can come up with an excuse, I'm going to have to come to terms with the fact that I'll be working with Rosie very closely for the foreseeable future.

I roll over onto my back and groan again. I stare at a water stain on the ceiling, tracing the dark outline of it with my eyes until I have it memorized. My mind jumps back and forth. I could ask to work with someone else, citing a conflict of interest, or just say that I won't work with her. I could put someone else in charge of these campaigns. I could hire another firm.

Every possible solution that I come up with falls short. She's the brains behind the campaign, that much is clear. If I refuse to work with her then I basically refuse the campaign. If I put someone else in charge on my end, I can't guarantee they'll deliver. If I hire another firm, I'm doing my clients a disservice.

I can't see any way out of it. I'm going to have to work with Rosie, and somehow forget the way her body tastes and smells, somehow forget the look on her face when she's in the middle of an orgasm, somehow forget the days and weeks I spent staring at my silent phone and feeling like a fool.

With a deep breath, I make my decision. I'll work with the Lockwood firm. I sit up and prep for the next meeting, even though my mind is made up. It's the best decision for my clients, that's why I'm doing this.

I try to ignore the part of me that fills with excitement at getting to see Rosie again.

20

ROSIE

I'VE BEEN STARING at a blank screen for ages. I'm numb. He hardly even looked at me, and couldn't get away fast enough. He practically ran out the door before I could say anything.

What would I even have said?

Congratulations, you're a father!

Please.

I sigh and put my elbows on my desk, resting my forehead in my hands. This is awful. Not only is he the father of my child and he doesn't know it, but this whole mess has probably lost me the biggest opportunity of my career. When will I get the chance to lead this type of campaign again? Especially if I have a kid to take care of.

The tears start gathering behind my eyelids and I take a few deep breaths to try to stop myself from bawling at my desk. I don't know how long I'm sitting like this when Harper's voice pulls me back to the present.

"You okay, Rosie?"

I look up and see her leaning against my cubicle wall, concern lining her face. I sit up a bit straighter.

"Yeah."

I can't think of anything else to say. Harper glances around and pulls a chair over.

"Are you sure? You don't look okay."

She sits down and leans forward, taking my hand in hers. I close my eyes and the tears spill down my cheeks.

"It's just…" I whisper. I pause. I can't tell her Lucas is the father. She'll tell Zach, and then they'll blame me for losing them the account. I look up at her and see her face lined with worry. "It's nothing, Harper. I'm just worried about the baby.

She puts a hand on my arm and squeezes gently.

"It'll be okay," she says. The words are frustrating instead of pacifying. How could this possibly be okay?

I nod and force a smile. "Thanks," I reply weakly.

"I have another meeting, let me know if you need anything. I mean it, Rosie, anything."

I nod and ignore the lump in my throat. She walks away and my hands shake as I dial Jess.

"Jess," I say as soon as she picks up. "He's here. He was in the office. Oh, God!"

"Who?" I can hear the panic in her voice. "Who, Rosie?"

"Lucas. It's the guy from my birthday. The father. He's hiring the firm. He's *here.*"

I hear Jess blow out the air from her lungs. She takes a deep breath in.

"The agent? The one you and Harper were talking about? With all the pop star clients?"

I nod. "Yeah."

"What do you mean? How is that possible?"

"I don't know!" I exclaim. I take a deep breath and lower my voice, cradling the phone against my shoulder. "I don't know. He was flying out that morning, he was going back to Los Angeles. I had no idea what he did for work."

"Are you going to tell him?" she asks in a hoarse whisper. I can hear the concern in her voice even through the phone.

"What would I say, Jess? How do you tell someone that? Someone you don't know? I tried to have half a conversation with him today and he basically ran away. He doesn't want anything to do with me."

"He was probably just surprised, Rosie," her voice is almost motherly and the tears start welling up again. "Maybe give him a call? You have his number now."

I shake my head. "You should have seen the look he gave me, Jess. He was disgusted with me. How can I tell him I'm pregnant? And I've probably lost the firm that contract. There's no way he'll hire us. And then Harper came over and I had to lie to her. How could I tell her it was him? Zach would go nuts!"

Jess is silent for a few moments and then she sighs. "Don't worry about the firm. Zach'll be okay, especially now that McKinley & Lee are out of business. Harper was just saying the other day that it's busier than ever." She pauses for what seems like forever and my heart sinks. "All you need to worry about is that baby inside you," she continues. "You owe it to him to tell him, and then let him decide what he'll do with the information. And Rosie," she pauses.

"Yeah?"

"You should tell Harper. She'll understand. Of all people, she should understand."

I laugh. "You're right. I'll just wait until he tells us he can't hire us."

"I wouldn't be so sure," Jess's tinny voice comes over the phone. "He might be drawn to you and hire you just to be nearer."

I snort. "Not likely."

Jess laughs and we hang up the phone. She's right, I have

to tell Harper, and I have to tell Lucas. I'll drive myself crazy if I start keeping secrets from everyone.

I spin my chair around and once again I'm staring at my computer screen. I open the email from yesterday and look at the footer. Lucas Thorne. His phone number is right there, all I have to do is pick up the phone and call.

My hands are shaking and my heart is thumping, and I haven't even touched my phone. I can't do this, not now.

I'll wait till he tells us he's not hiring us and then I'll tell him. It's cleaner this way, and it won't interfere with our professional obligations. Once he refuses our proposal, I'll tell him he's the father of our child. Easy, right?

21

LUCAS

YESTERDAY AND TODAY have been torture. I had two more meetings with different advertising firms and my fears were confirmed. Their proposals were subpar, not even coming close to the quality of Rosie's package. I sat through both meetings with a sinking feeling in my stomach.

I have to hire Lockwood's firm. I have to work with Rosie. I owe it to my clients and nothing can change that fact.

The clock says it's 4:45 pm, which means I have fifteen minutes to call Zachary Lockwood and tell him he's hired. I have fifteen minutes to lock myself in to six months of constant communication with Rosie, constant torture of seeing her and hearing her voice and knowing that she doesn't want anything to do with me. Constant reminders of her rejection, and of that nagging feeling inside me that I still want her.

I close my eyes and I see her, laid out on her sofa in front of me. The image has been burned in my mind since that night two months ago.

"Argh, stop!" I yell to my empty hotel room. I jump out of

bed and pull at my hair, bending over and pushing all the air out of my lungs.

I stand up again and rush to the desk at the other end of the room. I pick up my phone and in a couple seconds it's ringing.

"Lucas." Zach Lockwood answers on the second ring. "I was worried you'd forgotten about us."

"Not likely," I say, trying to hide the bitterness in my voice. "I've reviewed your proposal and I have a couple notes, but I'd like to move forward. I'll send through the contract in the morning and we can proceed from there."

"That's great, really great. We have a talented team. You'll love working with Rosie, she's one of our best editors."

My throat tightens and I nod, as if he could see me. "Right. Okay, thanks Zach. I'll be in touch."

I hang up as he's answering and throw the phone back down.

It's done.

Collapsing on the end of the bed, I hold my head in my hands and let out another sigh. I have no idea if that was the right decision. It could be the stupidest thing I've ever done in my life, just putting myself in an awkward situation for the sake of professionalism.

I don't even know if it's professionalism. It was the best proposal, sure, and my clients will benefit. But how much of it was because I actually *want* to see her again. I want to talk to her, to laugh with her, to get to know her? Even being in the same room as her today gave me a buzz.

As much as I try to deny it, I'm still drawn to her. I still want her.

It's wrong. I need to get myself out of this situation. If I have to work with her for the foreseeable future, I'll drive myself bat shit crazy.

I pick up the phone again and dial my boss.

"Linda," I say into the receiver.

"Lucas, how did it go?"

"Basically what I told you this morning. Lockwood has the best proposal by far, and I've told him we're ready to move forward."

"Great news. Good work, Lucas, you've saved our asses once again."

"Yeah, listen, Linda, I'm hoping this will be enough to let me stay in LA. I'm not happy spending so much time traveling. I want to be nearer to my daughter."

There's a pause on the other end of the line. I can almost see her lips purse, her hand smooth over her hair as it's always pulled back into a low grey bun.

"Lucas, we need you over there. You have the contacts and the know-how. This deal wouldn't have happened without you."

"Linda, you're not listening. My daughter is more important. Anybody can do this! Jake would be perfect. He's young and has nothing tying him to LA."

She sighs again. "I'll think about it."

"Alright. I'll send the contract through tomorrow and let you know how the meetings with Lockwood go."

"Talk to you soon."

I throw my phone down and lie back on the bed. So much for my exit strategy.

My phone rings and makes me jump. Allie's name pops up on the screen.

"Hi Dad!"

"Hi Allie," I answer, sitting back down. "How was your day?"

"It was great. But are you okay? You sound sad."

I sit up straighter and try to brighten my voice. "I'm okay, kiddo. Just tired from work."

"Okay," she says. She doesn't sound convinced. "Are you going to be in New York for long?"

"Not too long, Al. Just a couple more days and then I'll be back." Back, and away from Rosie and this head-melting situation. Back home, to my daughter.

"Okay." She starts telling me about her day and I ask her questions when I'm supposed to, but my heart isn't in the conversation. I take a deep breath.

"I have to go to bed, Allie. I'm falling asleep here."

"Okay. Hope you have a good sleep!"

"Me too, kiddo. I'll talk to you later."

I hang up the phone and sigh. It feels wrong to be rushing to get off the phone when I'm speaking to my daughter. It feels wrong to be distracted and unhappy when I'm talking to the person that matters most to me, when I should be enjoying every minute. It feels wrong to be almost disappointed that I'll be leaving New York when my daughter is on the other side of the country, and the woman I can't stop thinking about doesn't even want me.

It feels wrong but I can't help it. I'm attracted to Rosie— no, I'm drawn to her. It frustrates me and drives me insane but I can't deny that I still want her, as much as I wanted her when I first laid eyes on her in that taxi.

I want her, and I can't have her. Not only did she show me she's not interested, but now we'll be working together. If she hadn't shut that door three months ago, I've definitely shut it now by signing this contract.

It was a fling, a one-night stand, nothing more. She's an attractive woman and even if I still want her, I can't have her. I have to get over it and move on, for my sake and my daughter's.

I'll get this contract squared away and then leave New York. Hopefully, I won't have to be back for a long while and I can get my head straight again.

22

ROSIE

"TEAM, can I get everyone's attention?" Zach walks into the main room of the office and heads start popping up from cubicles like groundhogs. Harper walks out of her office and leans against the doorway. Our eyes meet across the room and she frowns slightly before turning toward her husband. She obviously doesn't know what he's about to say.

When everyone is looking at him, Zach speaks again.

"I'd like to congratulate everyone for putting in such a huge effort these past couple days, and one person in particular." He turns toward me and my heart sinks when I realize what that means. "Rosie, the work you've done has been outstanding, and has just landed us the biggest contract in the firm's history."

Cheers and clapping sound out through the room and a coworker puts his hand on my shoulder in congratulations.

The biggest contract in the firm's history. Lucas's contract.

Zach keeps talking about working hard and this being just the beginning. Typical manager talk and I zone out.

For the second time today, I'm numb.

He didn't refuse my proposal, he accepted it. He'll be

working with us for months and I'll have to spend god-knows-how-many hours with him.

I'll be working with a man who hates me, who just happens to be the father of my child.

Great.

I look up from my desk and Harper is there. Her eyes are wide and she's smiling from ear to ear. She opens her mouth as if to speak before Zach appears at her side.

"Excellent work, Rosie. We couldn't have landed this contract without you."

I nod, still feeling empty. "Thanks, Zach. I guess all that extra time I spent messing around with other people's campaigns finally paid off."

I laugh, but it sounds weak and thin even to me. Zach smiles and turns to Harper.

"You want to grab some lunch?"

Harper glances from him to me and I nod. I can tell she wants to stay with me but she can't say anything without telling Zach everything about the pregnancy. If only she knew that Lucas was the father. How can I possibly tell her now?

"And Rosie, you'll come out tonight to celebrate?"

"Sure, Zach, that sounds good. You guys have a good lunch."

Harper smiles at me and nods. The two of them turn away and I get up, grab my bag, and head to the bathroom. I go into the first stall and lock the door, put the toilet seat cover down and sit on it.

The dam bursts and all of a sudden, I'm sobbing. The tears stream down my face and all I can do is grab my stomach and cry. My face contorts and I feel the pain of a thousand knives pierce through my chest. I cry and cry and cry until my whole body aches, and then I cry some more.

When the tears finally stop, I take a deep breath and wipe my face with the rough toilet paper. I shake my head. For such a fancy advertising firm all they can afford is single ply.

Throwing the tissue in the toilet, I finally get out of the stall and see myself in the bathroom mirror. My face is red and blotchy and the tip of my nose is shining like a light. My eyes are puffy.

I splash water on my face and try to cool it down but nothing seems to help. I try to touch up my makeup and hide it as best as I can but I still look like hell.

Sighing, I turn toward the door. Hopefully I can escape the office and head home without anyone asking too many questions. Just as I'm about to come out, the door swings open and Zach's assistant, Becca walks in.

"Rosie, are you okay? What's wrong?"

"I'm fine, Becca. Just feeling a bit under the weather."

She looks at me and says nothing, just nods and steps out of the way. The look she gave me said *I know that's a lie, but I've been there.* Before I step out, she clears her throat.

"If you need anything…"

"Maybe just let Harper know I've gone home."

"Sure."

And with that, I shuffle out the door and duck out of the office. I can't face anyone right now, especially not coworkers.

23

LUCAS

THE PHONE RINGS and I sigh. My alarm clock says 7:22 am, and I should be up and ready for work. The beers I had last night are making my head pound, and my mouth feels like I've been eating cotton balls.

I know I shouldn't have drunk anything but I had to do something to blow off some steam. Rosie's face kept going around and around in my head. It still is, even after a night of one too many drinks.

I feel around the nightstand for my phone and look at the screen. I don't recognize the number but I press the green button anyway.

"Hello?" My voice sounds groggy even to my own ears.

"Oh, Lucas, I'm sorry. I thought you'd be up."

I shoot up right away when her voice comes through the receiver. I sit up in the bed and rub my eyes, trying to sound more awake.

"I'm up! I'm awake!"

There's a pause, and then a soft chuckle comes through the phone. "Okay," Rosie continues. "Well, in that case have you got a couple minutes? I thought we could talk."

My heart starts pounding in my chest. Talk?

"Yeah, sure, sure," I say, standing up and scanning the room for some water. "What do you want to talk about?"

"Well," she starts. Her voice sounds light over the phone but I think I can hear some hesitation. She breathes in and I hear the soft exhale she lets out. I wait, forgetting about the water and my headache and my cottonmouth and everything except what she's about to say. She clears her throat. "You want to meet for coffee?"

The words surprise me. I glance at myself in the big mirror on the wall and immediately start panicking. My hair is sticking up in every direction and I look like I've slept under a bridge. My eyes are lined and I smell terrible.

"Uhm..." I say.

"You know what, it's okay. I'm sorry, that was presumptuous. Are you available to come into the office? Maybe this afternoon?"

"*No*," I almost yell into the phone, and then cringe at my own awkwardness. "I mean, no, it's okay. Coffee sounds great. I'm just a little busy right now. I can meet you in an hour?"

"An hour is perfect. We can meet at BrewHaus near the office? It's just a couple blocks away."

"See you then."

We hang up and I let all the air out of my lungs. She wants to meet, to talk to me. Is this purely professional? It didn't sound like it, it sounded like she had something on her mind.

What if she wants to start talking, or even seeing each other?

What if she wants to tell me we should keep this professional? Break up before we even had anything?

I don't even know what I want. I want to grab her and kiss her and make every night like our first one, but I also want to tell her that she can't just ignore me like she did. I want to let her know how terrible she made me feel and how I don't care that she's the most attractive woman I've ever seen, she can fuck off for all I care.

That's not how I feel though. I don't want her to fuck off. I want her to stay by my side from now until forever.

My reflection is still staring back at me and I finally shake my head and snap out of my daze. I need to get ready.

After a steaming hot shower to scrub the last hints of alcohol away, I make my way to the coffee shop Rosie mentioned. I take a cab and stare out the window, trying to figure out how I feel, or what to say. More than anything, I just want to be near her. I glance at the seat next to me and remember the way she looked when her leg was extended toward me, her foot in my hand. I look out the window again and take a deep breath.

We pull up to the curb and I pay the driver before stepping out. I straighten my clothes and take a deep breath and then head toward the cafe.

The door jingles as I walk in and the smell of coffee hits me. I stand a bit taller and scan the room, trying to spot her at one of the tables. I look for her red hair, curls cascading around her face. My heart is pounding and my throat feels tight.

She's not here yet. I glance at my phone and see I'm a few minutes early, so I might as well grab a coffee and wait. Just as I take a step toward the counter, I feel something on my arm. I look down and see a delicate hand with four fingers placed on my forearm. I can feel the heat of her fingers through the fabric of my shirt, and my eyes trace the line from her fingers up her arm toward her face.

Her eyes are shining as she looks at me and suddenly, I'm speechless. Her lips look as pink and plump as they did the first time I saw her and immediately I know I won't be able to be mad at her. I can't even speak. There's a question in her eyes and she looks as nervous as I feel.

She smiles shyly and her tongue darts out to lick her lips. My cock starts throbbing as I watch it wet her lips, and I wish it was my own tongue tasting her.

The seconds seem to slow down and she slips her hand off my arm. The spot where it was feels empty and cold and I turn toward her. She opens her mouth again to speak.

"Hey," she finally says. It comes out barely above a breath but it sounds as loud as a freight train to my ears. The corners of my lips tug upward.

"Hey," I respond. My mind starts spinning as I try to think of something else to say. "You... you want a coffee?"

Her smile widens. She dips her chin down and tucks a strand of hair behind her ear. My cock throbs again.

"Sure."

24

ROSIE

EVERY TIME I SEE HIM, he looks better than the last time. The way his white shirt is stretched across his chest makes my whole body hum. He moves fluidly, turning toward me and taking a step in my direction so that all I want to do is wrap my arms around him.

His lips tug upward into a smile and my heart thumps. He's exactly how I remembered. He's just as broad and strong and manly, just as handsome as the first night.

"You want coffee?" he asks and I have to smile.

"Sure," I respond. It's all I can manage to say in between shallow breaths, trying to ignore the hammering of my heart against my ribcage.

I'm not even sure what I want to say to him. Jess thinks I should tell him, but now that he's one of our clients I'm not so sure. If he freaks out and pulls out of the contract, how would I explain that to Zach and Harper? I would have lost the firm's biggest client the day after we signed him. With a baby on the way, I need to make sure my job is as stable as possible.

He takes a step back and extends his hand toward the

counter, gesturing me to go ahead. I tuck my chin down and walk by him, inhaling silently as I walk by. He smells exactly as I remember—fresh and musky at the same time. I keep my eyes on the menu above the baristas and try to walk without stumbling.

He's so close to me it's making my head spin. He puts his fist on the counter and looks up at the board, and I slide in beside him. The heat of his body is making my head spin. I can feel his arm against mine, so close to me all I want to do is slide in and rest my head on his chest.

"What can I get for you?" the young man with a nose ring asks after he places someone's steaming cups of coffee on the ledge.

"I'll have a large green tea, and," I turn to Lucas.

"Americano, please."

"Nice," I say with a smile. "That's my drink."

Lucas smiles and frowns at the same time. "Not green tea?"

"Oh," I respond as I wave my hand. "I can't have coffee right now."

"Why not?"

Oh shit. Uh. Umm. Because I'm pregnant with your child?

"Doctor's orders," I respond and turn back to the barista and hand him some money to avoid Lucas's questioning stare.

"I'll get this," Lucas says as he reaches for his wallet.

"Please, my treat," I reply, and he nods.

"Thanks."

We stand in silence until our drinks are ready and then sit at a table near the front window. I stare at the people walking by until I feel Lucas's eyes on me. With a deep breath, I meet his gaze.

"Thanks for meeting me," I say.

"No problem. You seem nervous," he says with a slight frown. He lifts his cup of coffee up to his perfect lips and I watch his Adam's apple bob up and down as he swallows. I gulp.

"Just... surprised, I guess. To see you." *And be pregnant with your child.*

"Don't worry, I don't bite," he says with a grin.

"What if I wanted you to bite?"

The words slip out of my mouth before I can stop them and my heart starts jumping again. Each heartbeat sends a pulse through my center as Lucas's eyebrows raise ever so slightly. He stares at me with those pale blue eyes, trying to read my face. Why would I say that? We work for him now.

I drop my eyes and take a sip of tea. I know why I said that. I said it because the minute I laid eyes on him all I could think about were his hands on my body and his mouth on mine. Sitting across from him is torture.

Lucas clears his throat and shifts in his seat. I shouldn't have said that. I glance back at him and he's staring out the window.

"So, I, uh," I don't even know where I'm going with this, I just started talking without thinking. Why does he have this effect on me? "I'm glad you chose us to represent your clients."

His eyes flick back to me and the brightness in them dulls. Shit. I shouldn't have started talking about work. He nods.

"You were the best team. I look forward to working with your company."

His voice is empty, like he's suddenly lost interest. I don't know what to say to get the spark between us back.

"Thanks," I respond lamely. "So do we." He glances back out the window and I wring my hands together. This isn't me. I'm not nervous. I sip my tea again and feel my throat closing up. The thumping in my chest hasn't quieted down at all.

He takes a sip of coffee and sets his cup down gently. He folds his hands in front of it on the table and leans in. My heart starts hammering even harder. His eyes find mine and he searches my face for a few seconds.

"Why am I here, Rosie? Surely it's not to talk about work?"

I hardly hear his words over the heartbeat in my ears. I should have thought this through better, thought about what I wanted or what I should say. A thousand thoughts fly through my mind.

I'm pregnant.

Congratulations, you're a dad!

I have a surprise for you.

No its just about work, I wanted to discuss the advertisements in more detail and move forward with the campaigns.

I stare at my paper coffee cup and thumb the cardboard sleeve that surrounds it. I play with the tea bag label and fold it between my fingers.

"I just..." I pause, too nervous to look at him. With a deep breath, I lift my eyes up to his. "I just wanted to see you."

He looks surprised, and leans back in his chair slightly. His eyes leave mine and glance out the window again and I feel like a fool. I shouldn't have asked him here. What was I expecting? That he'd run into my arms and propose after I told him I was pregnant? I must be delusional.

He turns back to me and I drag my eyes up to his face. If he's going to reject me, I might as well face it head on. I let my eyes roam over his chest, his neck, I notice the way his shoulder muscles round out toward his arms and finally look up over his lips, his jaw and up to his eyes. There's something in his look that surprises me, a lightness, or a spark. The corner of his lip pulls up ever so slightly and my heart does a cartwheel.

"I'm glad you called," he says with his voice barely above a whisper. "I wanted to see you, too.

25

LUCAS

ALL MY ANGER and indignation at being ignored and rejected seems to have disappeared instantly. She's here, she called me, she wanted to see me. This wasn't a work meeting. It wasn't a way for her to clear the air. She just wanted to see me.

Why didn't you call?

The words are on my lips and I desperately want to say them. I want to ask her, demand to know why she ignored me for months and then all of a sudden now she wants to see me. It doesn't make sense.

A little voice at the back of my mind is nagging, eating away at me, saying that she's only doing this to smooth over our relationship for professional reasons. She's not any more interested in me than she was before, she's just doing what she can to make the professional relationship work. She doesn't care about me.

God, I'm pathetic.

Here's a woman, a beautiful woman, who clearly wanted nothing to do with me and I've been pining after her for months. She shows me the slightest bit of attention and I'm wrapped around her little finger.

I shake my head. I can't listen to that voice. Not now, not with Rosie sitting in front of me with that shy smile on her face. Not when her hand crawls forward a few inches and everything in my body is telling me to put my hand over hers.

I can still feel the spot on my arm where she touched me when we walked in. What would it feel like to touch her skin again? To taste her lips again? To taste between her legs again?

Why didn't you call?

The words hang between us but I can't bring myself to say them.

Instead, I move my hand so that my fingertips are just brushing hers. She inhales deeply and my cock throbs when her lips open slightly. Her eyes are still staring at me and I can't look away. She moves her fingers a fraction of an inch closer to mine and I do the same. We pause, staring, feeling each other's skin.

It's the smallest touch but it's sending a thrill up my arm. It's like her skin is made of fire and it's setting my veins alight.

I want more. I move my hand forward and interlace my fingers into hers. Her face breaks into a smile and her eyes are shining.

"I'm happy you're here," she whispers.

I never knew words had such power. I never knew that such a simple sentence could cause my whole body to burst into fireworks, cause my cock to pulse against my pants and my heart to jump out of my chest.

"You want to get out of here?" I ask.

She doesn't answer, only nods her head down once. I smile and stand up. I let her walk in front of me and open the cafe door for her. Her body looks amazing in those work clothes. She's wearing a tailored jacket and the most perfect pencil skirt I've ever seen. I could stare at her walking in front of me all day. We turn down the street and I'm just about to take her hand in mine when a woman's voice calls out in front of us.

"Rosie?"

Rosie stiffens and looks up. "Becca, hi." The woman comes closer and I recognize her from Rosie's office. The receptionist, I think.

"Becca, this is Lucas Thorne. We were just meeting to discuss the campaign." I almost burst out laughing but manage to keep a straight face.

"Right," Becca responds, glancing from me to Rosie. "Nice to see you again, Mr. Thorne. Rosie, I've been trying to call you all morning. Zach wants to see you immediately."

Rosie glances at me. "Immediately?" She asks, looking back at Becca.

"Yeah. He's waiting in his office. I was just getting him a coffee. You want one?"

"No thanks, Becca, I'm alright."

"Okay, see you up there. Glad you're feeling better."

Feeling better?

"Thanks."

Becca walks off and Rosie glances at me. She purses her lips and shrugs one shoulder up.

"Duty calls," she says. "Can I see you tonight?"

"Of course," I say. My whole body tilts forward a fraction of an inch and all I want to do is crush my lips against hers. I know we can't, not here. Not so close to her office, in the middle of the street. Knowing that I can't kiss her only makes me want to do it more.

Rosie lifts her hand up and squeezes my arm, just above the elbow. She smiles.

"Got to go. I'll call you later."

"You'd better," I say and she smiles. I doubt she knows how much I mean it. She stands there and her hand comes up to rest on her stomach. I nod to her hand.

"You feeling okay? We don't have to meet up tonight if you don't want to."

She drops her hand and shakes her head. "I'm fine. I want to see you tonight."

A smile breaks across my face and I nod. She smiles and her eyes shine before she turns away and heads toward her office. I watch her walk away and I hail the first cab that comes by.

I spend the whole cab ride staring out the window, just like I did on the way here. Except, instead of being nervous and filled with worry my heart is jumping for joy. She wanted to see me. She's going to call me tonight.

I replay the whole thing in my head over and over, burning the details of our conversation in my mind.

26

ROSIE

THERE'S a bounce in my step as I make my way back to the office. He wanted to see me! The way he grabbed my hand sent shivers through my whole body. I could almost taste his lips whenever I'd look at them.

My whole body is buzzing and I practically bounce into the office. Usually I'd be nervous about Zach calling me in for a meeting but right now, nothing can bring me down. I march across the main room, past all the cubicles toward his office.

I pass by Harper's office and I see her look up out of the corner of my eye, but I don't stop to talk to her.

All I want to think about is the fact that I'll see him tonight. He *wants* me to call him.

Zach is sitting at his desk when I knock on the door frame. He looks up.

"Ah, Rosie! The woman of the hour. Come in, close the door."

I do as he says and take a seat in one of the plush chairs across from his desk. He tents his fingers under his chin and looks at me for a few seconds before smiling.

"Harper always said you were one of our best editors but I

never saw by how much until just recently. The work you did for Thorne's clients is exceptional."

"It's not done yet," I reply. "We haven't even launched anything yet."

"That's why I wanted to call you in here. I know I asked you to lead the campaign's creative department, but how do you feel about being the editor in chief?"

My jaw hangs open. "I... I mean... really? What about Mitch?"

Zach waves a hand in front of his face. "Mitch has a lot on his plate. This is completely separate, and it's a clean break from our other work. It's the perfect opportunity to up-skill you and give you a chance to showcase your talents. We need a new editor-in-chief to run the music and entertainment clients and I think you'd be a great fit. If you do well with the Thorne file, we can talk about adjusting your title and pay to suit the new role."

"Wow, Zach," I start. "Thank you."

"Great! So that's settled. Talk to Harper about financials, and we're going to need a full timeline by the end of the week. You've got some good mockups so make sure they're fleshed out with more detail. I'd like to see two more ad sets prepped by tomorrow and a full proposal for the end of the week."

"I..." Zach looks up and cocks his head to the side.

"Is that okay?"

"Yes, yeah, of course. That's fine. Thanks, Zach."

He nods and I stand up to leave. I walk back to my desk in a daze. I've just been unceremoniously promoted. I've gone from senior editor to editor-in-chief in an instant, and my workload has quadrupled.

Harper materializes next to my desk.

"Zach told me," she says. "Congratulations!"

She's smiling but I can tell there are a million unspoken questions behind her smile. I nod.

"Thanks. I'm supposed to talk to you about financials."

"Are you free at 4:30 this afternoon?"

I glance at my calendar and nod. "Sure."

"Great, come to my office then."

She walks away and I lean back in my chair. A 4:30 meeting means a late night, especially when we're about to launch a huge ad campaign. I sigh. I was hoping to get away early and go see Lucas. I told him I'd call, and I desperately want to see him. But what can I do? I have to work, and this is a golden opportunity that won't come again. I've just been promoted, and I have a baby to think about. I have to prove myself.

I pull out my phone and find his number. The first thing I did this morning was save it in my phone.

Rosie: Hey, just got hit with a lot of work and a late meeting this afternoon. Might need a rain check for tonight, unless you're free around 9 or 10? Blame your clients 😊.

I press send and put my phone to the side. I hope he understands that work is important, even if he doesn't know just how important it is. A pay raise and a promotion would be a huge relief right now with a new baby on the way.

A baby on the way. It's so weird to think about it, to imagine what my life will be like a few months from now. I wonder if Lucas will be a part of it?

My hand brushes my stomach and I look down, wondering what my baby looks like right now. My hand drifts up toward the scar on my lower ribs and then up to the one near my collarbone. I remember the way it felt to have Lucas's lips on them.

I wonder if he'll want this baby, if he'll kiss my stomach the way he kissed my scars, or if he'll leave me to fend for myself. He could very well tell me that he doesn't want it, and I'll be in the exact same position I'm in now, except without the small flame of hope that I won't have to do it alone.

Just as the thought crosses my mind, my phone buzzes.

Lucas: No problem. I'm leaving tomorrow for LA, come grab a nightcap after work. We can complain about my clients together.

I smile .

Rosie: Sounds good, see you tonight. xx

I can't tell him about the baby, not yet. It's too nice to spend time together and to get to know each other. Tonight I just want to hear his voice and feel his skin and press my lips against his. I'll tell him soon. As soon as the time is right and I work up the courage.

Soon.

I turn back to my computer with a new lightness inside me. I'll see the father of my child tonight. I can just enjoy our time together a little bit longer before I break the news to him. I just want to enjoy this.

27

LUCAS

EINSTEIN WAS RIGHT ABOUT TIME, it's definitely relative. The hours have crawled by so slowly I wonder if the universe is broken.

I was disappointed when Rosie texted me, but I just keep thinking about seeing her later. We won't have very much time together, but that never stopped us last time. We had one night together before, and I already know how much we can accomplish in just a few hours.

I pace up and down my hotel room and wait for the time to pass. I finish my work, I do a short workout, I shower, I try to read and keep myself busy.

Finally I can't take it anymore and I head down to the hotel bar. I'll have some food and a drink and wait for her there. It's nearly 8 pm, surely, she should be done soon.

Time doesn't seem to speed up when I'm eating and I can't stop glancing at my phone. It feels like before, when I was just waiting on her to call. This time I'm just waiting on her to show up.

My food tastes like nothing and my drink is bitter, so all I do is sit and wait and read the news on my phone.

This is torture.

It's torture up until the moment that I feel two hands on my shoulders and I smell her perfume. Her hands slide down my arms and she slips into the bar stool next to mine. I glance over and can hardly breathe.

She's still wearing her work clothes but she's let her hair down. Her eyes look tired but bright, and her lips are wet. She slides her tongue over them and they glisten in the dim light of the bar.

"Thanks for waiting up," she says. Her voice is low and gravelly and my cock jumps in response. It's throbbing already and all I want to do is plunge it deep inside her. I could bend her over the bar, hike up her skirt and push her panties to the side and then just drive my cock into her right now. It wouldn't matter who was around or who saw, because nothing on Earth matters except for her.

"No problem," I manage to say, trying not to imagine her naked body or the way her nipples feel when they're between my lips. "You want a drink?"

"Not really," she replies. She glances at my almost full drink. "But I can have a soda water or something."

I shake my head, calling the bartender over for the bill. "No. Let's get out of here."

She smiles and ducks her head down. I love watching her when she tucks her curly auburn hair behind her ear. The light catches it and it looks like a million different shades of red. I sign the bill and charge it to my room.

"Let's go," I say. My voice is hoarse and all I can think about is the rock hard cock between my legs. Rosie stands up and I put my arm around her waist, guiding her toward the elevators.

The minute the doors close, we're two animals. The past months of agony and rejection and attraction explode between us and I grab her, turning her around and pinning her against the elevator wall. I take her wrists in my hands and hold them up near her head, pressing my hips against hers. She moans and I take her lips in mine, and then drop her hands to pull her shirt out of her skirt and run my fingers up her sides.

She wraps her arms around my neck and grinds her hips toward me, my hard cock pressed between our two bodies.

The elevator dings open and we fall out. I grab her hand and we practically run toward my room. My hands are shaking as I slide the key card into the lock and push the door open. She closes it behind her and drops her bag, her blazer, and tears at her shirt. In just a few seconds she's standing in front of me wearing nothing but her bra and lacy thong, and I'm still struggling to unbutton my shirt.

She takes a step toward me and grabs either side of the buttons, ripping it open in one movement. Her hands run up my stomach and around my neck and she presses her body into mine.

I can't get enough of her. I unclasp her bra and let it fall down and groan when her breasts fall free. I take them in my hands and she moans in response before clawing at my belt buckle. My pants fall down and Rosie falls to her knees with them.

"Rosie..." I groan.

"Shh," she says as she pulls my boxers down to my ankles and grabs my shaft with her hand. I groan again as she starts stroking, and then gently hitting her lips with the tip of my cock.

"I've been dreaming about this for months," she says. My eyebrows shoot up and I wonder why she wouldn't have called me, but I can't say anything because right at that moment her lips part and she takes my cock in her mouth.

It's wet and warm and her moans vibrate against the tip of my cock in the most delicious way. I tangle my fingers into her hair and gently guide her head back and forth. She raises a hand to put it over mine on the back of her head and presses gently. I grip her hair harder and push her head toward me with a bit more pressure. She moans and presses my hand a bit harder until I'm pushing her onto my cock and she's moaning with every thrust.

I've never had my cock sucked like this before. The feeling is unreal. Her hair is curled around my fingers and she glances up at me with her eyes watering. I pull away and she pants.

"Are you okay?" I ask.

She grins. "Get back here."

She grabs my cock in her hand again and a second later it's in her mouth. I can't take it anymore. My whole body is on fire. Every time her lips move down my shaft it's a new wave of pleasure crashing over me.

"Rosie, I'm going to come," I say.

She moans in response and then it's all over. I'm flying over the edge, standing just inside my hotel room with the woman of my dreams on her knees in front of me. She sinks her fingers into my thighs and keeps her mouth on me until my cock stops throbbing and my body stops convulsing.

I take a step back and stumble, my pants and underwear still around my ankles. She giggles and helps me toward the bed.

"Rosie," I breathe. "That was insane."

"I've been wanting to do that for a while," she responds with a glimmer in her eye. I can't think of anything to respond. The two of us lie back on the bed. I'm still panting and my heart is racing. I roll over toward her and drag my fingers down her bare stomach. She shivers as I get closer to her mound, trailing my hand under her panties and through her slit.

"You're so wet," I breathe. She laughs again.

"I wasn't joking when I said I've been wanting to do that for a while."

My fingers start running up and down her slit ever so slowly. She makes the sexiest little moan I've ever heard and turns toward me.

"If you can make me come half as hard as you did just now, I'll be happy," she says with a grin. "Looked like you enjoyed that."

I laugh and nod. "I'll make you come twice as hard."

28

ROSIE

I FORGOT how good his hands feel. He slides his fingers back and forth and all I can do is moan and enjoy the feeling of his skin against mine. The second his hand glides down toward my center I can feel my whole body trembling. It's like I've been ready to explode before he even touched me.

With one hand on my slit, Lucas starts kissing my neck. His kisses just below my ear, down toward my collarbone and back up again. He crushes his lips against mine and our moans mix together as his hand moves back and forth over my bud.

This is wrong on so many levels, but I can't help myself. He's irresistible. Right now, it doesn't matter that we'll be working together for the next few months. It doesn't matter that I'm pregnant, that he's the father, it doesn't matter that he doesn't know it yet. All that matters are his hands, his mouth, his body.

He circles his fingers around my bud and my body trembles in response. He shifts his weight to press his body against mine and I sink down further on the bed. I close my eyes and focus on the thousand little thrills that are coursing through my body through every vein to every extremity. He groans as my hips buck toward his touch and then shifts his body.

The instant his mouth touches my clit I know I'm going to come. I won't last long with his lips and his tongue covering my opening, devouring me. He groans.

"You taste better than I remembered," he breathes.

I can't answer. My hips grind up toward his face and he brings his lips back toward me. I've never had someone eat me out like this. He's groaning and licking and sucking me in ways I didn't know were possible. Every time his mouth connects with my center, I feel the pulsing of my heartbeat more intensely.

Just like he did to me a few minutes ago, I wrap my fingers into his hair and grind myself into his face. He groans and I groan as the pleasure inside me intensifies.

I can't think. All that matters is what he's doing to my body, and how my body is aching in response.

With his mouth still toying with my bud, he slips a finger smoothly inside me. He groans as his finger slides in, glancing up toward my face.

"You're so wet," he says in amazement. I open my eyes and look down at him. Our eyes meet for an instant and I see the clarity in his piercing blue gaze. His lips pull upward into a mischievous grin and he dives back down toward my slit.

This time, when his tongue touches me my body reacts and his fingers find my most sensitive spot. In an instant, I'm flying over the edge, screaming and wrapping my fist into his hair, arching my back and feeling my body convulse and shake as the pleasure bursts inside me. My veins feel like fire and my voice sounds like it belongs to someone else. I grind my hips toward him and he groans as he feels me come.

I'm panting, sweaty, moaning gently as my body finally

starts to quiet down. Lucas looks up and stands up to his knees, dragging his fingers out of me. I shiver as he touches my bud with the very tips of his fingers. He grins.

"How was that?"

"Nnmmmffff…" is all I can manage. I open my eyes lazily and try to focus them on his face. His eyes are half-closed, scanning up and down my body. I let my eyes drop from his eyes to his full lips, his jaw, down his muscular chest all the way to his cock.

"You're so hard," I breathe.

Without answering, he moves his hand to his cock and starts stroking it gently. He reaches down to his pants and pulls out a condom.

Too late for that, I almost say before I stop myself. He slips the condom on and I bite my lip as he moves toward me, lifting a leg up onto his shoulder.

When he enters me, I remember what it felt like the first time we met. All the times I've thought about him late at night, all the times I've replayed our first night together were just a pale shadow of the real thing. His cock feels bigger, harder, thicker than I remember. My walls grip him so tightly that I can feel every movement he makes.

I remember him feeling good but I don't remember him feeling *this* good. As if he's reading my mind, he groans and leans down toward me, teasing my nipple as he slides himself in and out of me.

"You feel better than I remember."

"So do you," I reply. He smells musky and manly and it's almost intoxicating. I can't control my own body.

He lifts my other leg up onto his shoulder and I know it's all over. It only takes a couple thrusts for my body to contract around him and for the pressure inside me to boil over. I'm coming again, saying his name over and over as the orgasm sends me flying.

I open my eyes and Lucas is smiling. Our eyes meet and I enjoy the last waves of my orgasm just as I feel him get harder. His head drops back and I watch him orgasm, wrapping my arms around his chest and pulling him in toward me as he comes.

When we collapse on the bed beside each other, my heartbeat slowly returns back to normal. My eyes flutter open and I turn my head toward him. He groans and opens his eyes before trailing his fingers over and back across my chest. I inhale deeply, enjoying the softness of his touch.

"Your touch feels so nice," I whisper. "Almost as nice as that orgasm."

Lucas chuckles. "Almost."

We both fall silent and my eyes close. Our breath mingles and our limbs intertwine and I fall into the deepest sleep I've had in a long time.

29

LUCAS

MY ALARM GOES off and Rosie groans. I chuckle and slide out of bed.

"You're not a morning person, are you?" I ask, looking at her collapsed form on the bed. Her hair is splayed out around her head like a halo. She squints at me and groans again.

"Morning people shouldn't be trusted," she says before rolling over again. I laugh.

"Does that mean you don't trust me?"

"You're an exception." She glances at me from the pillows and I see the hint of that smile I love.

My smile quickly turns to worry as her face falls. She looks at the bed as if she's in a daze and then makes a noise somewhere between a whimper and a groan. Suddenly, she throws the covers off and sprints to the toilet. Before I can react, the door slams and I hear the distinctive noises of her vomiting violently.

"Rosie, are you okay?" She retches again and I try the doorknob. It's locked. I bang on the door with my fist. "Rosie!"

I hear a flush and then the sink. After another painful moment the door opens and her pale face appears.

"Rosie! What's wrong? Are you okay?"

"I'm fine," she croaks. She opens her mouth and I wait for her to speak, but she just shakes her head and looks away. I watch as a thousand emotions pass over her face and I put my hands on her waist.

"Rosie if you're sick, I'll take you to the doctor," I say gently. "I can catch the next flight."

She shakes her head and says it again. "I'm fine. I've already been to the doctor. I...." She pauses again and looks up at me. Her eyes search mine and her mouth opens again and I wait.

"... you got any mouthwash?"

Her words surprise me but I nod. "Oh, yeah, of course. Mouthwash just in that bag, and the hotel has a toothbrush you can use. I have my own."

"Thanks."

We both go into the bathroom and brush our teeth side by side. I glance at her in the mirror and she opens her eyes wide at me to make a face. I laugh, toothpaste falling down my chin. It's been a while since I've brushed my teeth beside a woman, and it feels good to be here like this. Every time I'm with her it's just... comfortable. It feels like I'm supposed to be here.

Before I know it, it's time for me to leave for the airport. I give Rosie one last lingering kiss and say goodbye.

"I have your number now, so you can expect to be annoyed with all my texts," Rosie laughs. I frown, but before I can ask her what she means my phone rings.

"Cab's here," I say, glancing at it. She pouts and I laugh, tilting her chin up and giving her a soft kiss. "Talk to you soon."

This time when I leave for LA, I have the same lightness in my step as last time. I have the same excitement in the pit of my stomach as when I met her two months ago, except this time I have her number saved in my phone.

My phone buzzes and I grin as I see her name pop up. My heart feels light.

Rosie: I had a good time last night. Safe flight xx

My fingers tap quickly at the screen.

Lucas: See you when I get back.

For the first time in... well, maybe *ever*, I'm actually looking forward to New York. The city that used to mean long work days and busy streets is now somewhere I want to come back to. I have to go back to LA and meet with my clients to assure them that their launch campaigns and advertisements are in hand, but as soon as I can find an excuse I'll be flying back to New York.

I GO STRAIGHT from the airport to the office and almost bounce inside. I'm whistling to myself as I head toward my office.

"You're in a good mood," Linda's voice calls out from across the room.

"New York has that effect on me," I shoot back to my boss.

She walks out of her office and leans against the door, one eyebrow raised. "It doesn't usually."

Her hair is pulled back in her signature grey bun and she looks completely put together, as usual. She's been my boss for fifteen years and knows me better than anyone. I chuckle and shrug a shoulder before dropping my bag just inside the door. "Lockwood is good. They had a proposal prepped and should have full ad sets ready for review by the end of the week. If we're lucky, this whole ordeal will just be a tiny blip in sales."

Linda nods. "Good work. Maybe that spring in your step is just relief."

I laugh. "Something like that." *Maybe it's just the afterglow of the four orgasms I had last night.* I glance at my phone and wonder if it's too soon to call Rosie.

Heading in to my office, I start taking my laptop out of my bag and setting it back up on my desk. Linda clears her throat and I look up, surprised.

"Didn't realize you were there."

"Listen, Lucas," she starts. Her voice is neutral and I can't read her face. "You've done great work this past while. Going to New York at the drop of a hat when you're a single dad isn't easy, and it's appreciated. I know you've been asking about the assistant director position and I'd like to offer it to you officially. We can discuss the pay and responsibilities, but this way you can delegate a lot of the east coast work to the junior agents and stay in LA more permanently. I know that you value your time with your daughter, and this is my way of saying I heard your request, and thanks for your hard work."

My stomach drops. This is what I've been wanting for the past year and a half, and Linda is offering it to me on a silver platter. *Assistant director for the biggest agency in LA.* My heartbeat is rushing in my ears. If it's what I've always wanted, why does it feel so bad? I look down at my desk and Linda clears her throat again.

"Lucas? I thought this was something you were working toward. We don't offer promotions like this very often."

I shake my head. "No, no, of course. Linda, thank you. This is what I've been working toward for as long as I can remember. Thank you."

Linda nods and turns to leave. "You can bring Jake with you to New York when you go for the first weekly review and introduce him to the team. He'll take over after that. I'll let you get settled and we can discuss particulars tomorrow morning. How about 9 am?"

"Sure, sure," I respond, still staring at my desk in a daze. 9 am. I have just over 18 hours to figure out what I want to do.

I sit down and put my head in my hands. This shouldn't be a hard decision. On the one hand, I have a huge promotion and more stability for my daughter. I have less travel and more money. On the other hand, there's Rosie.

Rosie.

I lean back in my chair and drop my head, rubbing my temples with my fingers. I wish she didn't have such a hold on me. Why is this even a question? Of course I need to take the promotion, I have no choice. To turn it down for the promise of a relationship with a woman I've met twice would be foolish and irresponsible. With Allie to think of, I can't do that. Never in a million years could I turn this down.

All the time I thought I would be spending with Rosie, the business trips I thought I'd have, the time to get to know her—that's all going to be someone else's time. I'll be on the other side of the country in a supposedly 'better job' just because I'll be making more money.

I open my eyes and see my favorite photo of Allie framed on my desk. Of course I need to stay. That kid has been through so much, from the death of her mom when she was just two years old and dealing with my grumpy ass. She's stuck with me with a smile on her face through it all. This promotion is a good thing.

So why does it feel so bad?

30

ROSIE

"So how was your night of passion with the old baby daddy?" Jess asks. Harper's head whips around toward me.

"He's here?" Harper asks, looking between Jess and I. Jess shoots me a look and I know I need to tell Harper about Lucas. It's not a great situation to be in when your boss is also your best friend.

We're sitting in my living room, the two of them on the couch and me in the chair across from them. They're leaning toward me with shock painted all over their faces. Our mugs of tea are sitting forgotten on the coffee table between us. I lift my legs up and cross them on the seat.

"No, he left. He was only here for a couple days."

"Wait," Harper says, holding up her hands. "Back up. So the, uh, baby daddy, was in town on business and he contacted you? How did you get in touch? I thought you lost his number. How do I not know about this?"

I look at Jess and she shrugs, picking up her mug of tea and refusing to make eye contact with me. She did that on purpose. I take a deep breath.

"Harper, I didn't know how to tell you before. I..." I falter, looking at the ground between us. Harper leans forward.

"What is it Rosie?" She looks at Jess. "What's going on? What are you guys not telling me?"

"It's Lucas."

I finally meet Harper's eye and her face is frozen. Her jaw is hanging open. She shakes her head. "Lucas. What do you mean it's Lucas?"

"I mean Lucas Thorne. The agent. The client. He's... he's the father."

"What?"

"I didn't know until I walked in the conference room. I swear Harper, I was going to tell you as soon as he refused the contract but then he accepted and I didn't know what to do."

"So you fucked him again? That was your solution? You slept with the firm's biggest client?"

I wring my hands. "It wasn't like that. I was going to tell him about the baby, I met him for coffee and then... I don't know." I look at both of them, searching their faces for some understanding. Jess nods but Harper's face is unreadable. I know she's thinking about the firm. I take a deep breath.

"Harper, do you remember when you and Zach started seeing each other? How there was just... *something*. There was something between you and you had to go for it even though it was putting your whole professional career in jeopardy?"

Harper shakes her head. "Don't bring me into this."

"Why not? It's exactly the same. I had one night with this guy and it was incredible, you know? Like it's the first time since the attack that I've actually felt like myself again. It's the first time I've felt safe. And then I got pregnant. And now it's just blown up in my face and, and..." the tears start welling in my eyes and Harper is by my side in an instant. She's rubbing my back and cooing in my ear.

"Of course, Rosie. Of course, I'm sorry. I was just thinking about work. I know what you're going through. I've been there." She pulls away and I can see the love in her eyes. My shoulders relax.

"So did you tell him?" Jess asks, leaning forward on the couch. I cringe.

"Well, no, I didn't exactly tell him," I say, not daring to look at Jess in the face.

"Rosie!" They exclaim in unison.

"I will," I protest. "I will. Just... in my own time. It was too good. I couldn't ruin the moment."

"And now he's back in LA?" Jess asks. Harper purses her lips.

"Yeah, back in LA for a few weeks. He should be back here in a couple of weeks to go through the performance of the ads."

"I would give you shit for sleeping with a client but I don't really have a leg to stand on," Harper says with a laugh. "I've done worse. What's more scandalous, the CEO or the firm's biggest client?"

"At least Zach knew you were pregnant right away," Jess says as she raises an eyebrow toward me. "The longer you wait the worse it'll get."

"I know, I know," I say. "I just... it's just hard, okay? And since when are you the responsible one?" I ask Jess with a laugh.

"Since you got knocked up and won't tell the father he's a father," she huffs, leaning back in the chair and grinning with one raised eyebrow. I try to keep my face steady but I crack into a smile and start laughing. Soon the three of us are doubled over with peals of laughter.

"I'm so glad I have you guys to laugh with," I say. "This would be so fucking hard on my own."

Jess shakes her head. "I'm not sure I should be hanging out with you guys. At this rate I'll be getting knocked up by a coworker any day now." She laughs. "And I don't want any of those guys to come anywhere near me."

"I blame you, Jess. You're the one who told me I needed to get royally Fucked with a capital F. This is on your shoulders," I grin.

"Me!" she exclaims, throwing her hands up defensively and laughing. "I told you you needed to get Fucked, I didn't say you needed to get pregnant!"

I shake my head. Lucas's face appears in my mind and my heart immediately feels calmer. "I don't know what it is about him, I just *like* him."

"I've never seen you like this," Harper says. She looks at me curiously before continuing. "You look all... dreamy-eyed. You're my sarcastic friend and now you've gone soft."

"I'm still sarcastic. And besides, you were the first to go all gaga on us," I laugh.

Harper nods. "So when is he back? Surely it won't be for a few weeks?"

"Nah, we have to get the ads reviewed and approved and then launch them and he'll be back for the first weekly review. So like, three weeks?"

They both nod. Harper goes into Harper-mode: "And are you going to do long-distance? How is this whole thing going to work? Are you going to tell Zach? Are you together?"

I throw up my hands. "Harper, Harper! Too many questions. The answer to all of them is 'I don't know.' Up until a couple days ago I didn't even know his last name. All I know is that he's the best lay I've ever had."

Jess looks at Harper and then back at me. She leans forward and her face softens. I see concern in her eyes that I've never seen before. When she speaks, her voice is soft.

"In all seriousness, Rosie, you have to tell him. He has a right to know and make his own decisions before the baby is born. By the time he's back you might even be starting to show. If not in three weeks then definitely by the time he's back the next time."

She nods to my stomach and I look away. I stare at the patterns on my rug and think about what she's said.

"I know," I finally admit. "I was ready to tell him at the coffee shop but then I saw him and I just... I just couldn't. He was looking at me with those eyes and then all of a sudden, it's like it sparked and we were all over each other. I didn't want to ruin it by telling him."

"It'll only make it worse the longer you wait," Jess says. "Now you have to wait three weeks unless you tell him over the phone."

"I'm not doing that."

They both nod.

"Three weeks then." Harper says. "And after that you have to tell Zach. He'll kill me when he finds out I knew and didn't tell him."

"Thank you for not telling him," I say, and I mean it. I know that she tells Zach everything, and it's a testament to our friendship that she'll keep this quiet until I'm ready.

"You did the same for me just over a year ago," she says with a wink before checking her watch.

"I have to go. The babysitter will be angry if I'm late again. I don't know how she hasn't quit yet, with the amount of last minute work we pile onto her."

"Probably all those last minute paychecks," Jess laughs. "I'll walk down with you. Call me if you need anything, alright Rosie?"

I nod and show them out. When my door closes, I let out a big sigh and slump back onto the couch. I know they're right, and I know I've been a chicken by not telling Lucas about the baby. It's not like me, I usually face things head on. Lucas just makes me want to be with him and I'm terrified this will change his mind.

My phone buzzes and his name pops up, as if he could tell I was thinking about him. It's a photo of him in a steamy bathroom, wearing nothing and covering his crotch with his hand. His body is glistening from the shower and he has a smirk on his face. A text comes through straight after.

Lucas: Thinking of you xx

I sigh and lean back on the couch, staring at the photo. I'd give anything to run my fingers down that body. I type back a quick response and open the photo back up. He looks so good. His body is chiseled and muscular in ways I didn't even know was possible. The grin on his face makes his eyes sparkle and I wish I could kiss those lips.

Three weeks.

I can do three weeks.

31

LUCAS

IT'S ALREADY 9 pm for me, which means it's midnight for Rosie.

Lucas: Go to bed, I'll talk to you in the morning.

She answers right away and I sigh, putting my phone away. We've been texting nonstop the whole day. I haven't told her that I won't be in charge of the Lockwood campaigns, or that my next trip to New York will be my last. I'll tell her when I'm there, and we can work something out.

Maybe it's better this way. We're not directly involved with work, so that leaves us free in our personal lives. Maybe this whole thing is a blessing in disguise. Maybe she'd even consider moving to Los Angeles.

I lie back and stare at the ceiling. Soft footsteps make me turn toward my door. Allie pushes it open and pokes her head through.

"I'm glad you're back, Dad," she says in a half-whisper.

"Me too, kiddo. Come here," I say and open my arms. She jumps up onto the bed and nuzzles into my t-shirt. I wrap my arms around her and kiss the top of her head. "You're getting so big!"

"Can we measure me tomorrow? I think I've grown a lot since last time."

I chuckle. "Sure thing, Allie. I think you have, too."

Allie lifts her head and puts her little hands on either cheek. "You look good, Daddy. Like you're happier than you were before."

"I got some good news at work. I won't be traveling so much and I'll be able to spend more time with you." I tickle her and she giggles and squirms until I stop.

"Really?" Her eyes light up and my heart melts. I've been selfish. This is where I should be, with my daughter. I nod.

"Yep. They're going to let me run things from Los Angeles and send other people traveling."

"Maybe you can come to the Mathletes competition! We're competing against the other top schools in the city. I'm going to be captain!"

"I wouldn't miss it for the world, kiddo. Why didn't you tell me about it earlier?"

Allie shrugs. "I didn't want to bother you."

I ruffle her hair and sigh. "You'd never bother me. Now come on, it's way past your bedtime. Get to bed."

She smiles and jumps down from the bed. "Door closed or open?" She calls out as she bounces toward it.

"Closed," I respond. She turns around and blows me a kiss.

"Goodnight, Dad."

"Night, Allie."

The door closes and I let out all the air in my lungs. I didn't know my own daughter was competing in a math competition. I didn't even know she was the team captain. This promotion is definitely a good thing. I just need to remember that next time I see Rosie and feel that crazy attraction I have for her. There might be enough room for both of them in my life, but Allie has to come first, always.

I pick up my phone and scroll through the messages Rosie and I sent back and forth today. She's witty and clever and makes me laugh when I least expect it. I know Allie would love her, but she lives on the other side of the country. I didn't even know what she did for a job, and she doesn't even know I have a daughter.

I sigh and shake my head. This fling, or this affair, or romance, or whatever it is, is way too complicated. I'm losing sight of my priorities—priorities I've had ever since Allie's mother died. She told me to take care of Allie and I swore on my life that I would.

I have three weeks to figure out what I'm going to tell Rosie. I can't do long distance, and I can't move to New York. Above all, I have to put Allie first.

In a few days I've saved my client's careers, I've gotten a promotion, and discovered that my daughter is practically a genius. I've also met the woman of my dreams and had the most mind-blowing sex of my life. I should be happy. I should be excited about the future and hopeful for my prospects. I should be proud of my daughter and happy that I'll get to spend more time with her.

Instead, I'm worried about what will happen. I'm worried about losing Rosie, about losing something I never even knew I wanted in the first place.

Three weeks.

I have three weeks to figure it out.

32

ROSIE

THREE WEEKS DOESN'T SEEM like a long time until you're waiting for it to be over. The days drag on even though I'm working from morning till night. I'm chained to my phone, my heart jumping every time it dings and Lucas's name pops up. There's a spring in my step and I feel hopeful about the future, hopeful about my baby and about Lucas.

He's finally getting here today. My whole body is buzzing with excitement. I haven't felt this giddy in a long time. I can't wait to see him, even if the first eight hours will be at work. I have to wear a mask of professionalism all day, but still. I'll get to see him and smell his cologne and brush my hands against his arm. We'll work shoulder to shoulder and spend all day together in the office and then rip each other's clothes off the instant we're alone together.

The thought of his skin against mine is making the desire pulse inside me already. I just have to make it through the day without soaking through my panties.

Easier said than done.

I'm sitting at my desk, keeping one eye on my screen and one eye on the elevators. My knee is bouncing up and down and my heartbeat is faster than normal. I smooth my hair down for the thousandth time and check my makeup in my compact mirror.

"You look great," Harper whispers from behind me. I turn around and blush.

"I'm so nervous."

"Don't be," she says as she squeezes my shoulder.

The elevator dings open and both our heads whip around to see who steps out. My heart starts pounding when I see Lucas's broad shoulders and perfectly tousled hair come into view. He scans the room and when our eyes meet, he starts smiling. He looks away and shakes his head, putting a neutral expression on his face again. A younger, blond man steps out of the elevator behind him. He scans the room as well with a curious expression.

"Well, he's happy to see you," Harper says with a grin and a raised eyebrow. I blush again.

"This is ridiculous," I say as I put my hands against my cheeks. "I'm blushing as badly as you now."

Harper laughs. "Not quite. I'm brutal." She winks and walks over toward the two visitors and greets them warmly before pointing them to the conference room. I gather my things and get ready for a long, torturous day of work.

I step into the conference room and the breath leaves my body. All I want to do is climb on top of him right now.

I can't, obviously.

He stands up and extends his hand. I slip my hand into his and the electricity shoots up through my arm and straight to my core. His eyes are laughing as his voice stays placid.

"Rosie, nice to see you again. I'd like to introduce you to Jake. Jake will be taking over from me, so we need to get him up to speed over the next couple days."

His words are like ice in my veins. "Oh," I say, slightly taken aback. I extend my hand to the man. "Hi Jake."

"Nice to meet you. Rosie, is it?"

"I thought you were going to lead this?" I ask Lucas, ignoring Jake's question. Lucas looks from me to Jake and nods.

"Change of plans." *I'll tell you later*, his eyes seem to say. I nod and paint a smile on my face.

"Well, let's get started then. Jake, have you seen the detailed ad sets that were sent through yesterday?"

I push the million thoughts flying around my head out of the way and focus on what I'm good at: work. All I want to do is ask Lucas what he means, where he'll be, if I'm going to see him again. Did he ask to be taken off the project? Is it because of me?

I try to focus on what Jake is saying but my eyes drift back to Lucas. He glances at me and then looks back toward Jake.

My heart starts pounding. He's being so cold. Maybe it was his choice to be taken off the project? Maybe he doesn't want to see me at all.

I hate being this insecure. I don't like myself when I'm like this, and it hardly ever happens. I need to get it together.

"Do you guys want a coffee before we get started?"

"That sounds great, I'll help," Lucas answers quickly. I nod and the two of us head out of the room.

"Sorry, I should have told you earlier," Lucas whispers as we walk toward the kitchen. I glance up at him.

"So, does this mean you're not coming back?"

"Let's talk about it tonight."

He keeps looking straight ahead as I try to search his face. I frown, but say nothing. We make coffees in silence and I make myself a tea. He glances at it.

"Still feeling under the weather?"

"What?" I frown.

"The tea. I thought you said you were drinking it because you were sick."

"Oh, right. Yeah. Just got used to drinking it I guess."

Lucas lifts an eyebrow and nods. "Let's get back to it. Can I take you out to dinner tonight?"

I feel my shoulders relax and Lucas smiles. "Sure," I respond. I brush my hand over his arm and hear the hint of a groan inside him.

"Don't touch me till we're out of here," he says under his breath. "I won't be able to handle it."

I move my hand to his ass, shielded by the kitchen cupboards and give it a gentle squeeze.

"Oops," I say with a laugh. He grins and shakes his head before running his own hand down my spine. He lets his hand linger over my ass and moves it further so that his fingers are almost between my legs. I groan and take a deep breath before grabbing the steaming mugs.

"Let's go," I say. He chuckles and nods, following me out the door. So much for not soaking through my panties.

33

LUCAS

IF I THOUGHT the past three weeks were long, they were nothing compared to today. Being in the same room as Rosie without being able to touch her was pure torture. It was easier being across the country.

Finally, not a minute too soon we wrap up for the day.

"You go on ahead," I tell Jake. "I'm going to head back to the hotel and probably just get room service," I lie.

"Alright, no worries. If you change your mind, I'll let you know what bar we're at."

"I'm not as young as I used to be," I laugh. "I can't party like you kids anymore."

"Your loss," Jake answers with a grin. He heads out the door and I sigh. Rosie is tidying the papers on the table and she looks up toward me.

"Room service? Is that what you meant by taking me out to dinner? A bit presumptuous, don't you think?"

I grin. "No. I'm taking you to Emilio's. Seven o'clock reservation. You want me to pick you up?"

She shakes her head. "I'll meet you there."

Rosie stands up straighter and closes her laptop. Her lips curl up into a smile and she looks me up and down.

"It's good to see you," she says.

"It's good to see you, too," I respond. I take a step toward her and then catch myself and clear my throat. "Let's get out of here," I say.

We part ways at the bottom of the elevator and I have to hold myself back from kissing her. She squeezes my hand subtly and then winks before walking away. I watch as her hips move from side to side and she glances back, shaking her head and laughing.

"Pervert," she calls out with a laugh. I shrug and laugh before turning toward the hotel.

I hardly have enough time to go to my room, shower, change and be at the restaurant by seven but it still seems like an eternity. I get there before she does and wait at the table, ordering us both a glass of wine. The tables are candlelit and the restaurant is dim and cozy. I take a sip of wine to calm my nerves. I haven't felt this nervous around a woman since grade school.

I've spent two nights with this woman but this is our first date, and I'm as nervous as a teenager with his first girlfriend. I can't sit still and I can't stop looking at the door. I pull out my phone and flick through some apps before setting it down on the table. I hate being restless.

Finally, it opens and she steps through. Her black, skin-tight dress has a plunging neckline and shows off her milky white skin. Her hair looks like fire against the black of the dress and her smile is radiant when she sees me. She points to me and the hostess nods before leading her to the table.

I stand up and put my hand on her waist when she gets there, greeting her with a kiss. Our lips touch and my cock jumps. All I want to do is forget about dinner and take her straight back to my hotel. Instead, she pulls away and smiles at me before sitting down. I take a deep breath and sit across from her.

The candlelight flickers over her face and chest in a mesmerizing dance. Her eyes are bright and intelligent and she smiles as she lifts her glass.

"Cheers," she says.

"Cheers," I reply as I clink my glass against hers. Suddenly, all my conviction about staying in Los Angeles evaporates. It feels like this is where I should be, right here. She takes a sip of wine and I look at the way her neck curves, the way her hair cascades down in red curls and the way her breasts move ever so slightly with every breath.

I can't forget about her. I can't just turn my back on her. I haven't felt this way about a woman since my wife died, and I never thought I'd feel like this again.

There has to be a way to make this work.

"You clean up alright," Rosie says with a grin. "Who knew there was a gentleman under there."

My eyebrows shoot up. "Are you implying I'm not clean cut in the office?"

She tilts her head to the side and lifts her wine glass, looking me up and down. "I wouldn't say not clean cut, just... roguish."

"Roguish. What is this, a romance novel? Am I Fabio?"

She laughs. "It's not a bad thing."

"It doesn't sound like a good thing," I shoot back.

"It is, I promise. It's a very good thing." She takes a sip of wine and looks me up and down again. Excitement builds inside me whenever her eyes pass over me and my cock pulses in my pants every time she moves.

"So," she continues. "Tell me about this change of leadership. Why is Jake in charge of the campaigns and not you?"

"Not wasting any time, are you?"

"I'm a very direct person," she says.

"I can see that. I like that."

"You're stalling," she answers with a laugh. "I won't be fooled that easily."

I lift my hands up and nod. "Alright, alright. You're right. I... I got promoted. They're giving me the assistant director's position in the LA office. It's a crazy opportunity that I've basically been working my entire career to achieve."

Rosie looks at me intently and nods slowly. She takes another sip of wine and places her glass down gently. Her lips part and she looks me in the eye. Just before she can say anything the waiter appears.

"Are we ready to order?"

"Sure," Rosie says right away. She glances at me and then back to the waiter before placing her order. When he walks away, she looks at me again with that serious look. There's something else behind it, but I can't quite place it. She wants to tell me something. She looks at the candle on the table and then back at me, and the look is gone from her eyes.

"Congratulations," she finally says. Her voice is flat.

"What?" I frown.

"On the promotion. Congrats."

"Oh, right. Thanks," I respond. She smiles but there's a sadness in her eyes. My heart starts thumping and I feel like I've done something wrong. I rack my brain to try to think of something to say, but the words won't come.

I want to tell her that I want to see her, I still want her in my life, I don't want to lose her when I don't even know her, but nothing comes out. I clear my throat and take another sip of wine, and she does the same.

There's tension between us now. I know it's my fault. I haven't told her how I feel, or let her know how much she means to me. I haven't told her anything except the fact that I won't be back in New York. I don't know how to get back to the easy conversation we've always had together.

When she puts the wine glass down, she smiles at me. "Let's just enjoy ourselves tonight," she says.

I nod and smile. "Sounds good."

The words catch in my throat and I look at my half glass of wine. I might need another one before I'm ready to lay it all out for her and tell her how much she means to me. I take a deep breath and meet her eye again, trying to relax and let myself smile. I have all night to tell her I want to try to make this work. She's right, we should just enjoy ourselves.

"Cheers to our first date," I say, raising my glass.

She laughs and my heart sings at the sound. "Cheers."

34

ROSIE

MY MIND IS RACING. He's gotten a promotion, and he's handing off the campaigns to his coworker, which means he won't be coming back to New York.

Just when I thought we had some time together, just when I thought I'd be able to get to know him and tell him about the baby the right way, I find out that I don't have any time at all. He's on a flight out of here tomorrow evening. I have less than 24 hours to tell him he's the father of my child and then he leaves back to LA, back to his fancy life and big promotion.

Good for him. Congratu-fucking-lations.

My hands are shaking as I bring the glass of wine to my lips. It feels wrong, even though the doctor told me a glass of wine per week was alright. I stare at the dark red liquid and let it wet my lips.

"Good wine," I say as I put the glass back down.

"It is," Lucas answers. He stares at me from across the table, the candlelight flickering across his face. "I thought you didn't know anything about wine," he adds with a smile.

I look at my glass, swirling the liquid in it. "It's just something to say, isn't it? Does anybody know anything about wine? Are you sure this didn't come out of a box?"

"I did watch the waiter pour it, so I'm fairly sure."

"Doesn't mean anything," I say with a wave. Lucas laughs.

My heart is thumping and my stomach feels heavy. I'm not sure I can do this. It feels good to just laugh with him. It's so rare that I feel comfortable around anyone, and he's the first person I've been able to open up to in over a year. The thought of ruining that is breaking my heart already.

But, it's now or never, I have to tell him about the baby tonight. Otherwise I don't know when I'll see him again. At least if he reacts badly, I'll only have one more day of work with him and then he'll be on the other side of the country.

A thousand thoughts fly through my head. What if he doesn't believe me? What if he doesn't think it's his? Do I have to wait until it's born to get a DNA test? What if he gets angry? What if he yells?

What if he's *happy*?

That thought scares me almost as much as the others. If he wants the baby, and he wants to be part of my life, what does that mean? He's just gotten a promotion, but so have I. I don't want to leave New York to go somewhere I've never been, where I know no one. He wouldn't expect me to up and move, would he?

I take a deep breath and pick up the glass of wine again. With one more sip I'm able to sit up straighter and look at him again.

He's looking at me curiously, head tilted to the side and eyes squinting slightly. Even in the dim light I can see how piercingly blue they are. He licks his lips and my stomach does a flip.

Even with all these thoughts I still can't get over how attractive he is.

"Are you okay, Rosie? You seem worried."

I nod. "I'm okay. I just..." I pause. *I just want to tell you something.* "I'm just a bit sad that I won't see you again after tomorrow."

"We don't know that," he answers slowly.

"Don't we?" I shoot back. I hate how bitter I sound. He glances at the table and grabs one of the uneaten dinner rolls in the basket between us. He tears it open with his hands, reaching for the butter. I wait for him to speak, but he seems completely enthralled with his bread. I take a deep breath.

"I'm sorry, Lucas. I was just hoping we would have a bit more time together. I haven't met a man that I'm into in way too long."

He glances up at me and grins. "So you're into me?"

I snort. "Is that a serious question? Isn't it obvious?"

He shrugs and goes back to his dinner roll. "When you didn't call me when I left the first time, I thought you weren't interested in me. Like I was just a fling or whatever."

My heart starts thumping when his eyes flick up to mine and I see the hurt in them. The words tumble out of my mouth. "I lost your number. I can't believe I never told you this! It was on the paper and I brought it to lunch so that my girlfriends could help me text you and—"

Lucas starts laughing and I pause, mouth still open. "You needed help texting me?"

I blush and grab a dinner roll of my own. It's still warm and the steam billows out of it when I tear it open. I shrug. "I was nervous."

"I wish you'd told me you lost my number when you saw me," he says gently. "I waited for you to call for a long time. When I saw you again, I thought you weren't interested in me at all."

My heart starts thumping again, but instead of anxiousness, it's excitement building inside me. He *likes* me.

"I was a mess when I lost it," I say shyly, glancing down at the bread in my hands. I reach for the butter and smear it over both halves of the roll. "I wanted to talk to you so bad and I couldn't find you *anywhere* on social media. Are you a hermit?"

Lucas sits back and laughs. His shoulders relax and he shakes his head. He slides his hand across the table and I bring mine to meet his. Our fingers interlace and I feel the warmth traveling up my arm as he smiles at me. His eyes soften and the thumping in my chest gets heavier.

"I have to keep a low profile because of the job," he explains. "The artists like their privacy and if I was all over the internet it would hurt my career. Anonymity is safer. I wish I'd known you were looking for me."

I shake my head. "Well, we're here now. And we have less than a day before you leave again."

He looks pained and he nods. "Let's make the most of it." He glances up and around the restaurant. "I might head to the bathroom before the food gets here."

He stands up and ducks across the table, placing a soft kiss on my lips. It's warm and electric and sends a shiver through my whole body. When he pulls away his eyes are shining brightly and he winks.

"Be right back."

I smile and watch him walk away. He wanted to talk to me! He thought I rejected him and that's why he was cold when we first saw each other last time! I pop a piece of bread into my mouth and sit back as I chew. The bread is warm and doughy with deliciously melted butter all over it. I groan in satisfaction.

Something buzzes on the table and I notice Lucas's

phone. He must have left it on the table. I glance over and see a message flash across his screen. I look up toward the washrooms to see where he is. I can't help myself. The curiosity is too much. I lean forward and read the message as the screen lights up.

Allie: Love you! Can't wait to see you tomorrow.

My stomach drops and my heartbeat starts rushing in my ears. Who is Allie?

He has a girlfriend. Or worse—a wife. He's here on business, just telling me what I want to hear to get in bed with me again.

He wasn't waiting for me to call when he was in LA. Or if he was, it was just to make sure he had a piece of ass in every city he goes to.

I've been a fool.

My chest is heaving and my vision is blurry as my eyes fill with tears. He's played me. Of course he's played me. The fucking father of my child is having an affair with me. I can't believe I've been so *stupid*.

I wipe the tears off my cheeks and glance at the washrooms. He's still not there. I have seconds before he walks out and sees me like this, seconds before I make a scene in this restaurant and scream at him. I have just seconds to decide if I want all these strangers to see me at my worst, yelling at the lying, cheating bastard that happens to be the father of my child.

I can't do it. I grab my bag and rush to the exit.

It's not until I'm inside a cab that I let the tears flow freely. My hands are shaking and I can't even steady them enough to call Jess or Harper. It starts ringing as Lucas calls me and I quickly press the power button to turn it off. I just cry and cry and cry until the cab pulls up outside my house.

35

LUCAS

IT TAKES me a while to realize that she's gone. At first, I think she's just gone to the bathroom, and then I think she's doing her makeup, and then I think something must be wrong. I start looking around the restaurant and it's not until I see the waiter coming toward me that I start thinking that she's in trouble.

When the waiter asks me if I still want to eat my dinner, I don't understand what he means. When he looks back at the hostess and they exchange a look, my stomach starts churning. When he tells me she's gone, the ground falls away and my blood starts to rush through my veins faster than I thought possible.

I say something to him and he walks away, but I'm not quite sure what I said or what he replied. All I can do is stare at the table in front of me and try to process what's happened.

She's gone. Why? Why is she gone? She'd just told me that she wanted to see me even after the first time, that the only reason she didn't call me was because she lost my number.

I left to go to the bathroom feeling like the king of the

world and now she's just *gone*? My confusion turns to hurt which turns to anger. My anger bubbles up until the rage is gripping my throat.

I grab my phone. Allie's texted me and I swipe the message away. I find Rosie's number and dial it.

It rings twice and then goes to voicemail.

She hung up on me. I take the phone away from my ear and stare at the screen in amazement.

What the *fuck* is going on?

I dial her number again and it goes straight to voicemail, it doesn't even ring once. The anger intensifies inside me and I mash out a text message.

Lucas: Where are you?

I press send and wait for the little 'delivered' to appear under the message. I refresh the screen and still nothing. She must have turned her phone off.

I sit back in my chair and the waiter appears with big Styrofoam packs of food. I guess I told him I'd take the dinner to go. I nod and give him some money.

"Keep the change," I mumble as I grab the bag and stalk out of the restaurant. I glance up and down the street, half hoping to see Rosie coming toward me even though I know she won't be.

She's gone.

I start walking in the general direction of my hotel just as the skies open up and rain starts pouring down. I stop walking and look up, feeling my clothes soak through in seconds.

Of course. Of. Fucking. Course.

I can almost hear the rain sizzle as it hits my red hot anger. I walk through the streets toward the hotel with my shoes squelching with every step. I just don't understand why she would leave without saying anything. And then just cut me out and turn her phone off?

Maybe the whole thing about losing my number was a bunch of bullshit. She could tell I was mad about it and came up with some excuse, and then when she saw that I was into her she ran.

Coward. That's what she is, she's a complete coward.

I can't believe I fell for it *again*. Not once but twice with the same woman I get played for a fool. I think she's into me and then she just turns her back on me. Twice!

I walk into the hotel and keep my head buried in my chest as I make my way to the elevator. It's not until I'm standing under the hot shower that I let my shoulders relax down and I let the anger dim ever so slightly.

I haven't cried since my wife died, and it feels ridiculous to cry now over a woman I hardly even know. I still don't know how she's gotten under my skin or why I even care. She gave me a glimpse of something that was missing in my life and then just turned around and walked away. But here I am, a grown man sobbing in the shower over a woman he never even dated.

The shower washes away my tears and soon I'm able to breathe normally again. My anger fades slightly and I step out of the shower to towel myself off.

She's gone, and I'm going back to LA. I'll be with my daughter and I can put this whole chapter of my life behind me. I'm just embarrassed at being rejected twice by the same woman. I'll recover, I'll find someone else. Or else I'll find no one and I'll be alone. Either way it's better than feeling like this.

I pull out my phone to text Jake to tell him I won't make it in to the office tomorrow. If she's being a coward and running away from me, then I will too.

36

ROSIE

"It's probably not what it looks like," Jess's voice comes through my phone. "There could be a perfectly reasonable explanation."

"That's just the typical thing that people say to make themselves feel better when they find out something that is exactly what it looks like," I shoot back.

Jess chuckles. "Maybe. Or maybe he has a daughter, or a mom, or maybe Allie is a man! Who knows? The worst thing you can do is shut him out. He's your baby's daddy for crying out loud."

"Please stop calling him that."

"It's true. You have a baby daddy, and it's time to come to terms with it."

"Jess," I start.

"Rosie," she answers. I chuckle and I can almost hear her smiling on the other side of the line. "Come on Rosie, just pick yourself up and pick out a great outfit for work tomorrow. Send him a text to apologize and explain. Say you freaked out because you were moving too fast or something. Or just be honest and ask who she is."

"I thought Allie was a man," I say as I roll my eyes.

Jess laughs. "Not likely. Come on, Rosie. Chin up."

"Alright, thanks Jess."

I hang up the phone and I stare at the blank handset. I should text him. It was wrong of me to leave. Wrong and childish and hurtful.

Rosie: *I'm sorry I left. I freaked out.*

I hit send and cringe. God, I'm pathetic. I've seen the man three times in my life and I'm already running out and groveling to come back. What is wrong with me? My stomach grumbles and I realize I haven't eaten since lunch. I throw the phone down and head to the kitchen to make some dinner.

Cooking calms me down, and I force myself to stay away from my phone. Before I sit down to eat, I check my phone and frown when I don't see a response. I check the message—it says read, which means he's looked at it and hasn't responded.

That's understandable, I try to tell myself even as it stings to see it. I *did* walk out on him with no explanation, after all. He's allowed to have time to calm down. I'm sure he's mad at me.

But then again, he is the one who has been cheating on his girlfriend with me. *He* should be groveling to *me!*

I take a deep breath. I'm going to drive myself nuts. At least I get to see him tomorrow at work. Maybe I can catch a few minutes with him alone and work it all out.

It's NOT until I get into work and see Jake that my heart really sinks. Lucas isn't coming in today, which means I won't see him at all before he leaves. Not unless he answers my message and agrees to meet before his flight.

The day crawls by and his silence is deafening. Harper

notices and keeps shooting concerned glances my way but I pointedly ignore her. It's not until Jake leaves to catch the plane that I realize it's all over.

It's over.

I'm a single mother, and the father of my child is a deadbeat who knocked me up while having an affair. He probably saw the message and realized that I knew about Allie and that's why he doesn't want to see me. He knows that he's a scumbag.

That's what I tell myself all the way home to stop from breaking down. That's what I say to Jess when she calls, and when Harper comes over that's what I tell her too.

He's just a jerk. He didn't deserve me. I'll raise the baby on my own, I don't want that kind of man in the kid's life anyway.

The more I say it the easier it is to believe. The voice that screams in my head telling me I'm wrong gets quieter and quieter until it's easy to ignore it. I can ignore the thoughts that say he's different, he's worth fighting for.

He's not.

He's just like all the others. A liar, a cheat, a coward. He couldn't even face me head-on. Harper listens and nods and I see the sadness in her eyes.

"I'm sorry, Rosie, I thought he was different. You deserve better."

Even she knows the script. I nod. I deserve better.

"Yeah, I do deserve better. He's not different, none of them are," I say bitterly. "Except Zach, obviously."

Harper chuckles. "There are some good ones, Rosie, don't lose hope."

"Who's going to want to be with me now?" I say, looking down at my stomach. "Pretty soon I'll be blowing up like a balloon and I might as well have a neon sign with me that says 'COMES WITH EXTRA BAGGAGE.'"

Harper's laughing now. "Rosie, stop. It's a kid, it's not a life sentence. Well," she pauses, "It is a life sentence in a way, but a good one. The right man will be happy to take on both you and your baggage."

The tears well up in my eyes. "You think so?"

"I know so. Zach is no angel. He ran out on me too when he realized he was a father."

"Yeah, but he came back," I respond. Harper stays silent. "Thanks for coming over. You shouldn't be over here, you have a husband and a baby daughter at home, you should be with them."

"Stop, Rosie. You're my best friend and you're going through a hard time. Zach is perfectly capable of being a father and changing a few diapers."

"Thank you." It comes out barely above a whisper. She wraps her arms around me in a big motherly hug and I feel a little bit less alone.

37

LUCAS

YOU'D THINK it would be easier to get over Rosie's rejection the second time it happens, but it isn't. The days turn into weeks and I slip into my new job without any major issues. Linda is happy, Allie is happy, and I pretend that I'm happy too.

Every time I see a redhead my heart skips, and then I hate myself for it. I cling onto my anger like a lifeline, remembering how much she's hurt me whenever I think of how much I miss her.

It gets easier as time passes.

BEFORE I KNOW IT, six months have gone by and I'm clapping my hands as Allie beams on stage. She steps forward to accept the trophy for the state-wide Mathletes competition and scans the audience for me. I wave and shout, clapping my hands together even harder. She looks toward me and smiles before raising the trophy above her head.

"That's my daughter," I say to the woman beside me. She smiles and nods and claps along with the rest of the parents.

Allie is ecstatic. She runs toward me once the ceremony is over, holding the medal around her neck in both hands.

"Look, Dad! Look! It's so shiny."

"Well done, kiddo. I didn't even know the answers to any of those questions, you are some kind of genius."

Allie elbows me and stares at the medal, tracing the engraved design with her finger. "Thanks for coming, Dad."

My heart melts. "I wouldn't miss it for the world, Allie." I put my arm around her and kiss the top of her head.

"I'm glad you took the new job. I like having you here." She swings her arm around my waist and looks up at me. I wink and her face cracks into a smile.

The bitterness that's been inside me since I came back from New York disappears for a second. I squeeze her shoulder and she wraps her little arm around me a bit tighter. I hear someone clear their throat and I look up to see one of the mothers in front of us. She sticks her chest out and looks at me through her lashes.

"Congratulations, Allie," she says without looking at her. "You did a great job up there."

"Thanks, Mrs. Miller," Allie responds. Mrs. Miller is still looking at me.

"And you must be Allie's father," she says, extending her hand. Her nails are sharpened to a point and I try to avoid them as I bring my palm to hers. She squeezes my hand and takes a step forward, placing her other hand on my upper arm. She strokes it and gives me what she must imagine is a sensual smile.

"Nice to meet you," I say robotically, trying to take a step back.

"I haven't seen you around much," she says, eyeing me up and down.

"No, I'm busy with work. But I couldn't miss this," I say, looking down at Allie and winking.

Mrs. Miller nods. "Well, we're having a celebration this weekend at our place with all the kids and their parents. I'd be so happy if you could make it."

The words drip out of her mouth and she drags her eyes all over my body and up to my face. I feel almost naked, with a cold shiver running down my spine.

"Thanks," I respond. "I'll think about it. Come on Allie, we should go."

"See you Saturday."

"Right." I brush past her and bring Allie along. A year ago, I'd have been all over her. Objectively speaking, she's an attractive woman. She has obviously taken care of herself and isn't shy about showing her interest.

But now?

Now she's almost repulsive. I haven't been able to talk to a woman, let alone meet one that holds my interest longer than a couple seconds for months.

"Can we go?" Allie's voice floats up toward me. I look down at her and my eyebrows shoot up.

"Go where?"

"To the party! The whole team is talking about it. Apparently, the Millers have a pool."

"I'm sure they do," I answer. "I'll think about it, kiddo, I might have work to do." Allie nods but says nothing and I sigh. I should go, if only for her sake. I can grin and bear any conversations with Mrs. Miller or any other person at the party if it means Allie will enjoy herself. She deserves it, she's put up with a lot from me for a long time.

I open my mouth again and sigh. "I'll make some time for it, okay? It'll be a good way to celebrate your big win."

Allie's face breaks into a huge smile and I laugh. That's

the smile that I'd move the Earth for, the smile I'd cross oceans and deserts to see.

Well, one of the smiles. There's one other smile in this world that makes my stomach churn and my heart beat faster, but that smile might as well be dead to me. Even if she were beside me, I'm not sure I'd be able to speak to her.

Still, when Allie and I get into the car and I watch the other parents stream out into the parking lot I know that something is missing from my life. I watch couples help their kids into their seats and then get in the front, laughing and talking the whole time. I glance over at Allie who's still studying her medal. Have I been depriving her of a mother? Has my lack of interest in other women actually been hurting her? She tells me she's happy, but she's so quiet and she never asks for anything.

Mrs. Miller comes out of the theatre and heads toward her car. I feel no attraction to her, but I wonder if having someone like that in my life would be good for Allie, good for both of us.

I start the car and pull out of the parking lot. Maybe it's time to move on, for real this time. I have to leave Rosie behind me and look for something better for both me and Allie.

38

ROSIE

"THANKS SO MUCH, GUYS." My eyes are misting up as I look at my coworkers. They're smiling at me as they eat the cake that was brought in for me. Everyone signed a card and pitched in for a much too generous present comprised of dozens of different gift cards.

"This is way too much."

"It's nothing," Becca says as she smiles at me. "Just promise you bring the baby in for us to meet as soon as you can."

I grin. "Deal." My hand drifts over my stomach and I feel the smooth bulge of my belly. It seems like all of a sudden, the baby grew and grew and grew and now I can hardly walk without waddling. "Shouldn't be too long," I add, laughing. "I'm ready to get this baby out of me."

"You still don't know what it is?" One of my coworkers asks.

"No, I decided to do it the old fashioned way and wait till it was born. At least I can do that the old fashioned way if nothing else!" I laugh.

There's laughter and talking and everyone munches on

cake and enjoys the few minutes break they get from my office baby shower. I keep looking around and stroking my baby bump—well, more of a baby mountain stuck on my stomach—until Harper slides in beside me.

"I'm so proud of you," she says with misty eyes.

I can't help but laugh. "Proud? For getting knocked up? Everyone thinks I got dumped, and they're probably just doing this because they feel sorry for me."

Harper shakes her head. "Everyone chipped in because they like you, Rosie. We all want the best for you."

My throat tightens and Harper squeezes my forearm. The emotion makes it hard to swallow and I try to think of something to say that won't make me start crying. I can't think of anything, so I just say nothing.

I'm saved by Zach, who walks up beside Harper. She leans into him in an almost imperceptible movement and my heart twists slightly. I'm still jealous of how happy and comfortable they are. They're made for each other.

"You can't keep that thing in there for just a couple more weeks?" He asks. "We're going to miss you with this next launch."

"Zach!" Harper says, swatting his stomach with her arm. She gives him a look that drips with disapproval. Zach laughs and I can't help but join.

"Zach, I know you're my boss and you're the CEO and all that, but I can honestly say that right at this moment I don't give a rat's ass about the next launch. I have bigger things on my mind."

Zach grins. "That's why I like you, Rosie. You're not afraid to speak your mind."

"And you do have more important things to take care of," Harper adds. "Are you sure you don't need me to do anything for you?"

I shake my head. "I'm fine, really."

I'm fine, and I'm alone. I watch as Harper turns to Zach and he brushes his fingertips along her arm. The envy curls in my stomach as I watch them laugh at something unsaid, speaking to each other with just their eyes.

I want that.

I want it so bad and it's so far away. Who will have me now? I'm days away from giving birth, and then for almost twenty years I'll have a whole other human dependent on me. I don't feel the slightest bit ready for this.

I turn toward the cake and help myself to another slice. I try to chew in silence and quell the rising panic inside me. How am I going to do this on my own? I can barely take care of myself!

As if it can sense my nervousness, the baby kicks. It's a hard kick, right up into my ribs. "Oof," I breathe as I brace myself. "Alright, alright, I hear you," I smile as I rub my stomach. "We'll be okay."

I have no idea if other mothers talk to their babies like this. I know it can hear me and feel what I say. A part of me thinks it can understand me, even though the logical part of my brain knows it can't. It understands what I feel, in any case.

It's not until I get home and put my feet up on the coffee table that I let myself sigh. I let my thoughts drift to him. To Lucas. He never spoke to me after I walked out on him, and a part of me can't really blame him. He has no idea he'll be a father, and he has no idea how much I've thought about him over the past nine months, ever since the first day we met.

I've learned to deal with the sadness, but the loneliness still gets to me. I stroke my belly in long, slow strokes, feeling my baby as it lays inside me.

"You're tired, aren't you," I say to my stomach. "We had a

big day today. Don't worry, baby, you'll be out in the world soon and you'll be seeing new things every second of every day. I'll protect you. I promise."

My eyes well up with tears and I whisper it again. *I promise.* A fierceness grows inside me as I think about my baby being born. Of course we'll be okay, and of course I can do this, even if I'm on my own. I'll take care of this baby and help it grow into a healthy, happy child. I'll do anything for it. I know that already.

It kicks and I smile, tears streaming down my cheeks. "I love you too, baby. It's just you and me now."

39

LUCAS

"THE ALBUM LAUNCH LOOKS GOOD, and we just tweaked a couple things for the tour branding," Jake says. I look at the report he's given me, scanning the pages and half-listening to what he says. Ever since we hired the Lockwood firm, our sales on the east coast have skyrocketed. Rosie is talented, and even if I wanted to find another firm, no one would let me. It's not like I have to deal with her anyway.

"So yeah, all systems go," Jake continues. "It'll be interesting to see how the next few weeks go without Rosie leading it all, she was basically the motor for the whole project."

My head snaps up and I stare at Jake. "She's not working there anymore?"

"Maternity leave. Didn't I tell you she was pregnant? She looked massive a month ago, can't imagine what she looks like now. Ready to pop."

My whole body is frozen with shock and I can't even tell Jake to stop speaking about her that way.

Pregnant? Since when?

I mean, I know since when. Since approximately nine

months ago from now. But I've seen her since then, I *had sex* with her since then! Did she know she was pregnant when she saw me when we signed the contract with Lockwood?

"Lucas. Lucas?" My head snaps up and Jake is staring at me, frowning. "You okay?"

"Yeah, yeah. I'm fine. That's all for now, Jake. Thanks."

Jake looks at me curiously and opens his mouth as if he's about to protest and then changes his mind. He gathers his papers, nods, and slips out of my office quietly. He closes the door behind him and I let out all the air from my lungs. I bring my hands up to my face and rub it, making circles around my temples and rubbing my eyes.

She's pregnant.

Nine months ago... Nine months ago was going into summer. Nine months ago was June. I frown. I met her in June—that was the wild night we had together when I came back and thought she ignored me. When she 'lost my number', if I even believe that.

Nine months ago we had one night together.

No. Obviously not. It couldn't be.

My stomach churns. My head shakes from side to side and all I can say is *no, no, no*. Not possible. We used protection. I had a condom. I reach back into my mind and try to remember what happened that night. I've replayed it so many times in my mind it comes back easily. I used a condom, I'm sure of it.

We were on the couch, and we fell asleep. I had one of the best orgasms I've had in years.

I stand up and shake my whole body to try to relax. Pregnant? Could it... could it be mine?

No. Definitely not. No chance. Right?

But what if it was mine?

I sit back down at my computer and pull up a search

engine, heart pounding as I remember the sex education classes from years ago. My fingers tap quickly:

Condom effectiveness

I press enter and in a couple milliseconds there are thousands of results. I don't even need to click any of them—it says it right there in the preview. When used correctly, they're 98% effective.

My heart is thumping. Ninety-eight percent isn't one hundred percent. What if...

I can't even bring myself to think it anymore. I shake my head. We were careful, we used protection. It was one night. Sure, we had sex multiple times, but it was one night. She didn't even call me afterward. She never mentioned it when I saw her again.

It isn't mine. It can't be mine. I'm already a single dad, I've already had one kid, I can't have another.

My eyes flick to the picture of Allie that I keep on my desk. She was the best thing to ever happen to me, but another baby?

"*Ah!*" I yell out to myself. I'm going crazy. It probably isn't even mine! She never called me, and she never said anything. If it was mine, she would have said something. I stand up and grab the papers on my desk, ripping them apart in both my hands. I throw the scraps of paper and they flutter down harmlessly around me.

Like a movie montage, I think of every single interaction I've had with her. Refusing coffee, barely sipping her wine, clutching her stomach. Throwing up before I left for the airport. She wasn't sick. She was *pregnant*. She knew, and she didn't tell me.

I remember at the coffee shop, when she said she wanted to talk about something. Or our last dinner together, at that Italian place. The candlelight was flickering all over her face and she looked like she was tortured, like she wanted to tell me something and couldn't.

And then she ran away.

I slump back down in my chair, holding my head in my hand.

She ran away because I told her I wouldn't see her again, that I'd accepted a promotion and I wouldn't be back in New York. She ran away because I told her I was unavailable, that she wasn't important enough to me. She ran away because she couldn't bring herself to tell me that she was pregnant with my child, and then she tried to reach out to me and I left her out in the cold and didn't speak to her for six months.

I open my eyes and the weight of the world falls on my shoulders. That baby is mine, I know it is. That night she told me she hadn't been with anyone in months.

She was lying, they all say that. The angry voice in my head whispers in my ear. I push it away. I've listened to that voice long enough. Rosie wasn't ignoring me, or acting distant. She was terrified of telling me about the baby, terrified of my reaction. I reacted in the worst possible way without even knowing about it and she just protected herself.

Somewhere in New York, on the other side of the country, my second child is about to be born.

40
ROSIE

I'M IN A WEIRD LIMBO. I'm on maternity leave but the baby isn't born yet and all I have to do is sit around and wait. I rub my belly in big, circular motions and walk around my apartment, back and forth down the hallway. The doctor said being up and active helps induce labor.

There's a pile of presents in the corner of the living room, and an overnight bag packed for when I need to go to the hospital. Zach and Harper came over to help me build a crib and set up the bedroom, and the apartment is starting to look like it's ready for a baby. I have diapers of all different sizes, little onesies with funny sayings on them, wet wipes, baby formula in case my milk doesn't come in, tiny socks and little hats. I have Harper's old stroller and a thousand and one of her baby toys.

"We'll have to share a bedroom for now, little baby. I'll get you your own room eventually, I promise."

I've been promising the baby lots of things, and I'm not sure I'll be able to keep them. I've promised to keep it safe, to raise it properly, to do my best. I've promised to get it its own room and to make sure it never wanted for anything.

In truth, I don't know if I can provide for it. I'm completely, utterly terrified. In a matter of days, or hours, I'm going to be a mother.

I keep rubbing my belly and walking, breathing in and out and trying to ignore the thumping of my heart when I think about what's going to happen. My fingers reach the edge of my lowest scar, just on the bottom of my ribs. I touch the length of the scar and shiver as my fingers pass over the smooth skin.

Like a flash, I remember being on my couch—the one just in front of me here—with Lucas lifting my dress up and worshipping my body. He kissed me like I've never been kissed, he touched me like I would break if he grabbed me too hard. He traced every scar with his fingertips, and then his lips.

I sit down exactly where I was that night. I close my eyes and imagine him here, touching me like that. My fingers trace my scars one by one and I remember how vulnerable I felt with him, but how good it felt to be touched that way and to feel safe.

"That's the night you were created," I whisper to my belly. The baby squirms and I smile. "Yep, you might not want to hear that but it was that night. Right here where I'm sitting."

I keep tracing my scars one by one, laying back on the sofa until my eyelids get heavy and I fall into a deep, peaceful sleep.

THE CONTRACTIONS WAKE ME UP. I touch my belly and feel it completely hard and I panic for a moment before I remember the doctor describing exactly this. It feels like I'm being squeezed around the middle. It intensifies, and then goes back down. I look at the clock. 1:17 am. The contraction subsides and my stomach goes back to normal.

"You just couldn't let me have one last night of sleep, could you?" I sigh, and then smile. "I'm looking forward to meeting you."

The clock ticks onward slowly and I wait for the next contraction. It doesn't come for almost twenty minutes, but this time it's more intense. The pain grows until my face contorts and I cry out.

My breath comes in short gasps. 1:34 am.

When it passes, I grab my notebook from my purse and look over the scribbles I took at the doctor's office. When the contractions last 30-60 seconds and are 5 minutes apart I should head to the hospital.

1:44 am.

This time the squeezing is more intense, and the pain radiates through my whole abdomen. My back starts to ache and I groan, wincing as I wait for the pain to pass.

The night drags on like this, with me watching the clock like a hawk. The contractions are getting worse and worse and they are lasting longer and longer. There's a thin film of sweat all over me even though my apartment is cold.

I glance at the clock again. Six minutes. Close enough. I grab my phone and call a cab, sliding my jacket on and picking up the bag I've prepared earlier.

Harper demanded to know when I go to the hospital, but it's just before four AM. I'll hold off for an hour before I text her. I don't want her to rush over to me, it could be hours before I give birth. My fingers hover over my phone and I think of Lucas. My heart squeezes in its own type of contraction when I realize that I'm really doing this alone. I'm giving birth to our child and he doesn't even know it exists.

I find his number and my thumb hovers over it. If I just

move it a quarter of an inch, I'll tap the message icon and I can tell him what's going on. Then the ball will be in his court, and he can choose to be part of the baby's life or not.

My heart thumps in my chest, beating harder and harder as my thumb trembles over the button.

I almost jump out of my skin when the phone rings.

"Hello?" I answer, my voice low and scratchy.

"You called a cab?"

"I'll be right down." I hang up the phone and slip it into my pocket. Maybe I'll text him later, when I tell Harper and Jess. For now, I need to make it to this cab before the next contraction hits.

41

LUCAS

I HAVEN'T SLEPT a wink tonight. I've been staring at the ceiling, tossing and turning. My mind is jumping all over the place and I can't get her out of my head. Rosie, pregnant with my child. I know it's mine. I'm sure of it.

I have to go to New York.

I don't care what it costs, or what Linda says, or how crazy it is to go over on a gut feeling, but I have to go. I have to see Rosie.

I'm sure that once I see her, I'll know if the baby is mine. Who am I kidding? I already know. I sit up in bed and run my fingers through my hair.

"I know it's mine," I whisper to the darkness. "I already know, I don't need to see it to know."

I throw the covers off and pace back and forth in my bedroom. If I'm much louder, I'll wake up Allie and I don't want to do that. I just pace back and forth, back and forth until the black night turns grey and the first hints of sunlight start appearing.

Pulling my bedroom door open, I head down to the

kitchen and put on some coffee. My laptop takes a few minutes to boot up and I hop from foot to foot.

"Come on, come on, come on!"

As soon as it's running, I start looking up flights. I could leave in three hours and be there in nine. I'd be there at 1 pm.

Just as the mouse is hovering over 'book', I take a deep breath. I don't even know if she's still home, let alone what hospital she'd be at. I don't even know if she's in labor yet. I didn't even know she was pregnant until a few hours ago!

"Dad?" Allie's voice makes me jump. I spin around.

"Hey, chicken. What's up?"

She frowns as she looks at me. "You look terrible."

I turn toward the big kitchen window and see my reflection for the first time. She's not wrong. My hair is sticking up in all directions and my face has lines in it I didn't know existed. I look old and haggard and like I haven't slept in a year.

"Couldn't sleep?" She says as she takes the coffee and pours me a mug. I take it from her and ruffle her hair.

"Thanks. Isn't it a bit early for you to be up?"

"I could hear you down here. Are you okay?" She tilts her head to the side and I see her mother in her. I sit down at the kitchen table and Allie comes up to me, placing both hands on either side of my face.

"I'm okay, Allie. Just lots on my mind."

"Is it Rosie?"

I pull back. "What?"

"Rosie, is that why you can't sleep?"

"How do you know about Rosie?"

Allie rolls her eyes in the way that only preteens can. "Dad," she says, putting her hands on her hips. "You were texting her nonstop for like, ever, before. And then you stopped and got all sad. I wasn't born yesterday, you know."

"No, I guess you weren't," I answer, amazed. Somehow my twelve year old daughter manages to surprise me almost every day. I take a sip of coffee to delay the inevitable barrage of questions. She doesn't let up.

"So is it Rosie?"

I chuckle. "You're just like your mother, you know that, Allie?" She lifts an eyebrow up and I can't help but grin a little bit wider. "Fine, yes, it's Rosie. I haven't spoken to her in a while but I think... I think..."

I can't say it. How can I tell my daughter that? How can I tell my daughter that I think I had casual sex with a woman and knocked her up and she might be a big sister? I don't even know for sure.

Allie tilts her head to the side and climbs onto the chair beside me. "What do you think? Is she in trouble?"

"No, not exactly," I respond.

"Does she miss you?"

"No. Maybe. I don't know."

"Do you miss her?"

"Yes." It's the first time I say it out loud and I can't even look at Allie when I do.

"Why won't you talk to her?"

"It's complicated, Allie. You'll understand when you're older."

Allie sighs. I finally look at her and her bright eyes are trained on me. "Dad," she starts. "What is it you always tell me?"

"That I love you and I'm proud of you?" I answer hopefully. I'm not feeling like the parent in this situation and I don't like it. Allie shakes her head.

"You tell me to be true to myself." She gets off the chair and pokes my chest. "What does it feel like in here?"

My throat tightens up and my eyes start misting. "She's

having a baby," I finally say. I wipe my eyes and see Allie's face staring at me, wide-eyed and smiling.

"I'm a big sister?" She almost yells.

"No," I blurt out. Her face falls. "I mean, yes, I don't know Allie. It's complicated. You shouldn't be listening to me at all. I shouldn't be telling you this. You're too young."

My daughter narrows her eyes at me and brings her nose closer to mine. She studies my face for one, two, three seconds and then finally pulls her head away and nods.

"Let's go."

"Where?"

"To New York. I want to meet my little brother."

"What? Allie, stop." She's walking toward the computer and I wonder when my little girl became so headstrong. "How do you know it's a boy? You can't come."

"Why not? And I just know. Now come on, let's go."

She turns toward me, sticking her chin up and looking at me. She balls her fists up and plants them on her hips. I see my stubbornness and her mother's determination written all over her.

The laughter starts in my stomach and bubbles up through my throat until my head is thrown back and I'm laughing with my mouth wide open. I wipe the tears streaming from my eyes and see Allie grinning up at me.

"Let's go," she says a bit more softly.

"I don't know how this has happened, but okay. Just this once, okay, Allie? We're not doing this again."

"Fine," Allie responds, but I see the glimmer in her eye that tells me she doesn't believe me. I don't know if I'm being a good parent or a bad one right now, but I can't say no to her.

Either way, even if it's crazy to pull her out of school and fly across the country with her, it feels right. She can meet

Rosie and her new sibling—brother, according to her—and I can make up for lost time. I might not have been there for the pregnancy but I sure as hell will be there for the baby.

42

ROSIE

Harper: On my way.

I sigh, knowing that Harper shouldn't be dropping everything to be with me, but at the same time relief courses through my veins. The contractions are getting more intense and even though I'm surrounded by doctors and nurses, I've never felt so alone.

I'm terrified.

The phone is sitting on the nightstand, taunting me. Lucas is one call away. How would he react?

I sigh. He would react like any sane person who gets a call in the middle of the night telling him he's hours away from becoming a father. He would freak out, obviously. I can't do that to him.

It's just these crazy pregnancy and labor hormones that are making me consider calling him now, of all times. I had six months to call him and tell him about the baby, and I never did it. I can't call him now. What would I even say?

Another contraction builds inside me until I'm doubled over in pain, panting and sweating as a nurse comes over and rubs my back.

"Good job, Rosie, that's it. Just breathe through it. They're getting more frequent now, I'll get the doctor to check you again in a bit."

I groan in response, not able to make words. The pain rises and falls like a tidal wave and I slowly straighten myself up again.

I've gone from pacing my apartment to pacing the hospital hallways. The woman who shared my room when I first arrived has already gone to give birth. Based on the relaxed look of the nurses around me, I'll be here a while.

I should have stayed at home.

Time drags on and on until I hear my name from down the hall.

"Rosie. Rosie!" It's Harper and Jess, and behind them Zach. They're carrying bags and pillows for me. Harper's face is flushed as she hustles toward me.

"Rosie, how are you feeling. Ah, I'm so excited. This is great!"

"Is it? It's more like agony than great, I'd say," I answer as I lean against the wall. I put both hands underneath my bulging stomach and take a deep breath.

"Looks horrendous," Jess says. I glance at her sideways and she grins. "Sorry."

"It's okay. I'd be saying the same if it were you in my position," I laugh. "So much for not having kids, hey?"

"Oh, come on," Harper says. "It's not that bad."

"Harper. You've been through this. How can you say it's not that bad?" I glance up at Zach and he grimaces. He remembers the screaming and swearing that went on when Harper gave birth to their daughter.

Harper shrugs. "However bad it is, it's worth it."

I nod. "I'm going to be a mom," I whisper, looking at my belly and giving it another rub.

"Yes, you are. Now come on, we brought you some goodies, where's your room?"

The four of us head to my room and I lay back down, groaning and sighing in relief. Jess plumps up my pillow and Harper holds up the million things they've brought for me. Pillows, pajamas, magazines, hand cream, things I'd never have thought to bring.

"You've done this before," I say to Harper. She laughs. "All the things I wished I had when I was here."

Her phone dings and she glances at it. "Oh!" Her eyebrows shoot up and she glances at me and then at Jess.

"What is it?" I pant. Harper hesitates. "Just tell me," I say.

"Lucas Thorne heard you were pregnant and has a gift basket for you. He asked to have it delivered either at your house or here at the hospital if you're already here. What should I tell him?"

I hardly hear a word after 'Lucas Thorne'. My heart starts thumping against my ribcage and another contraction starts. I turn to my side and double over as the pain intensifies. I groan louder and louder as it gets worse, willing it to be over. It lasts longer than any other contraction I've had so far and I wonder how much worse they'll get. It feels like an eternity.

Jess is stroking my hair and Harper holds my hand when I can finally relax. I open my eyes and look at Harper. "What did you tell him?"

"Who?"

"Lucas? Did you answer?"

"Don't worry about it Rosie, I just said send it here. There might be some nice treats for you once this is all over. I'll take care of everything, okay?"

"That's nice of him to send something," Zach says. "He must be impressed by your work."

Harper, Jess and I exchange a look. I never told Zach who the father was.

"What?" Zach asks, his eyebrows knitting together as he looks from his wife to me. "What did I miss?"

"Nothing, babe. It's very kind of him," Harper says.

I nod and close my eyes again, rolling onto my back. Jess pats my forehead with a damp towel.

A gift basket? What would that even mean? Why would he text Harper instead of emailing the office?

The questions fly around my brain and I can't make any sense of them. The minute I think I've come up with an explanation, another contraction starts and I'm in agony for another never-ending minute.

"Good work, Rosie, you're doing great," Jess coos into my ear. I open my eyes and look at her, not able to think of something suitably sarcastic to say. She smiles at me and squeezes my arm. I close my eyes again and wait for the next wave of pain.

The door startles me as it swings open.

"Sounds like someone's contractions are getting better. Or worse, whatever way you want to look at it."

I squint at the doctor, hating his cheerfulness. His grey hair and ruddy cheeks make him look friendly but I can't bring myself to feel anything except pain and misery right now. The doctor disinfects his hands and then claps them together.

"Well," he says. "Let's have a look, shall we? Legs up!"

I glance at Jess who glances at the doctor. He's altogether too cheery, but I do as he says and pray that he tells me I'm ready to get this over with.

43

LUCAS

ALLIE's little hand is in mine as we walk through the terminal and make our way to the taxis. We don't have any checked baggage, and she's wearing her favorite pink backpack that's almost as big as she is. She squeezes my hand.

"I'm excited!" Allie skips beside me. "I always wanted to meet Rosie. She seems nice."

"She is. But how would you even know?"

Allie shrugs. "I saw a message flash on your screen. She was saying hello. She just seems nice, the way she talks."

I say nothing, wondering why Allie never mentioned anything. Probably because I never did.

We walk the rest of the way in silence, and climb in a taxi. I give the driver the name of the hospital that Harper gave me before staring at Allie. She and I are probably not the gift basket she had in mind when she agreed to give me Rosie's hospital room.

We speed through the streets but it's somehow too slow. Allie's nose is glued to the window as she stares at the city. She makes noises and points at buildings as they race by. I smile. Maybe it's good that I brought her here, took her out of

LA to see something different. The cab weaves through the streets and as we get closer my heart starts beating faster.

I haven't seen Rosie in six months, and now I'm bursting in as she's about to give birth to a child that I'm not even sure is mine. What if the real father is there? What if I'm wrong and I burst in on their intimate family moment? I'll look like an idiot, and a creep. My career will be over, that's for sure.

I am a creep, asking for her location and then just showing up. That's the definition of creepy. God, what am I doing?

Before my thoughts can spiral out of control, Allie's hand finds mine and she gives it a squeeze. She smiles at me and nods slightly. I relax my shoulders down and smile back at her.

We're here now, and there's no turning back. If the baby isn't mine, if Rosie has someone else, if she's alone but she wants nothing to do with me—it doesn't matter. I'll have done my best to come here and let her know that I'm available. I want her, I want the kid, I want a family again.

We pull up to the hospital and I pay the fare before climbing out of the cab. Allie comes around to stand beside me, once again slipping her fingers into mine.

"You ready?" She asks.

"Not in the slightest," I respond, laughing. "I'm shitting myself."

"Swear jar!" She says as she pokes me in the ribs and laughs. "It'll be okay, Dad. I can't wait to meet my little brother."

"What if it's a girl?"

Allie shrugs one shoulder and looks at me, pressing her lips into a thin line. "It's not, but if it is, I'll be just as happy."

I laugh and shake my head. "Okay, kiddo. Let's go."

The glass doors slide open and we step through. The

reception desk is just to the left, with hallways shooting off in every direction. There's a waiting room to the right and a few people glance up as Allie and I walk in. I look at the boards to try to find the maternity wing before giving up and heading to reception.

"Hi, here to see Rosie Jackson."

The woman stares at me blankly. "Any idea what she's here for?"

"Right. She's uh—she's giving birth. She's having a baby. Maternity. Room 213 I think?" I stumble over my words and cringe at how awkward I sound. The woman doesn't seem to notice, she just nods and slides her glasses down to the end of her nose to look at the computer screen in front of her. She taps a few things and then looks back at me.

"Just down that hall, to the left. Take the west elevators to the third floor and then turn right. You'll see another set of elevators with maternity written above them. Take them to the second floor and that's where she is."

She frowns as she looks at the screen. "Looks like she's gone into the delivery room already. When you get to the maternity floor turn left and ask reception what room she's in, I don't have access to that information here. You'd better hurry or you'll miss all the action."

"All the... action?"

"Let's go." Allie shouts as she pulls my arm toward the elevator. "Dad, let's *go*!"

I'm in a daze. Even though I came across the country and found out where Rosie is and brought Allie, it's just hitting me now. Rosie is giving birth. She might be giving birth right this instant. I might see the birth of my second kid.

Something stirs inside me and all the doubt evaporates from me. I know this baby is mine. I can sense it in the depths of my heart, in the depths of my stomach, or my soul, or wherever. All I know is that it's mine. I don't know how I know, but as Allie pulls me down those stark white hospital hallways, I know that I'm going to be a father again any minute now.

My mind goes blank and my heart starts beating, sending waves of warmth through to every extremity. Allie drags me along and I float down the hallways, feeling like my body belongs to someone else and I'm just along for the ride.

We find the elevators, take them to the third floor, turn right, and see the big black words above the second set of elevators: MATERNITY. Allie jumps up and presses the 'up' arrow. She squeezes my hand and I look down at her, still in a daze.

I'm about to meet my second child. I'm about to see Rosie. I'm about to introduce them both to my other daughter. This is either going to be the best moment of my life or the undeniable, absolute worst.

44

ROSIE

THERE'S SHOUTING and sweating and swearing and grunting and I'm not sure what's my voice and what's everyone else's.

The pain is excruciating. I know I'm crushing Harper's hand, somewhere in the back corner of my mind I register my knuckles turning white and the tips of her fingers turning bright red, but all that I can focus on is the pain. The contractions are coming fast now and they are more intense than I could have imagined. It's like menstrual pain times a million.

The contraction subsides and the doctor pops his head up. "Okay, the next contraction it'll be time to push like you've never pushed before. Do you understand?" he asks. His cheerfulness has been replaced with complete focus.

"Get this baby out of me," I gasp between pants. The doctor grins.

"Yes, ma'am."

"And don't call me ma'am," I say before leaning my head back. Harper presses a damp towel to my forehead.

"You're doing great."

I close my eyes and feel the next contraction start building in the pit of my stomach. I can sense the wave of pain start to build and build and the nurse beside me lifts my shoulders up and grabs my other hand.

"Ready? Three, two, one, PUSH."

I've heard of 'bearing down', of 'pushing', I've read about childbirth, but nothing prepared me for the feeling I'm experiencing right now. I'm not sure if I'm pushing a baby out or trying to empty my entire abdomen of all my organs. My body is being torn in half. I hear myself scream as my face contorts, my teeth clamping down and tears streaming out of my closed eyes.

"That's it," the doctor calls out. "Keep pushing! Just a little bit more!"

My vision is going white and I think I'm going to pass out when the contraction starts to subside. The nurse pats my shoulder and helps me lean back.

"Deep breaths, now, Rosie. You're doing great. Deep breaths, in and out," she models the breaths for me and I try to follow her lead. My heart is hammering against my chest and the tears are still streaming out of my eyes. I breathe in, close my eyes, and blow the air out slowly through my mouth.

"That's it," she says, patting my shoulder. "Just keep breathing."

Just when my heartbeat feels like it's starting to slow down, I feel my contraction start again. I groan and open my eyes, lifting my shoulders up with the nurse's help.

"Okay, this is it, Rosie, you can do it."

They say pain is nothing, it's temporary and it's in the mind. But right now, pain is real, it's visceral, and it's never-ending. It twists through my stomach and sends arrows of agony through my veins. It wraps itself around my spine and squeezes me like a huge fist. It burns as it shoots through my entire body and all I can do is scream, swear, gasp, and push.

As if I'm underwater, I hear the doctor say something about the head. He's talking excitedly but all I hear is gurgling and many voices around me. Harper squeezes my hand and suddenly the pressure between my legs is relieved. The doctor slides his hands back and I see a glimpse of my baby through my blurry, tear-filled eyes.

"What is it? Is it okay?" I gasp, not understanding what's going on. The baby is handed off to a nurse who takes it to the nearby bassinet. The nurses and doctor crowd around and work quickly and efficiently as Harper stands next to me, squeezing my hand.

The seconds tick by and I lift my head toward them. "What's going on?" I croak again. The fear starts building inside me when no one answers.

Finally, relief flows through me as I hear the screams of my newborn baby. Its cries get louder and louder as the medical team works over it until the doctor steps back, beaming. My eyes are glued on the bassinet, tears still streaming down my face. My hair is plastered to my forehead and all I can do is pant and wait.

"Congratulations." The nurse smiles as she turns around and places the baby gently on my chest. "You have a beautiful, healthy baby boy."

The minute my son touches my chest an overwhelming wave of love fills me to the brim. I look at his little scrunched face and start laughing and crying and laughing some more. Harper strokes my shoulder.

"He's beautiful," she whispers. "Just beautiful."

"He looks like an alien," I laugh, looking at his lumpy head and wrinkly face. He has patchy, bright red hair all over his head. "But he's my little alien." I stroke his tiny arm with my finger and start laughing again.

I'm completely in love. I've never felt anything like it. I'm in a daze, and I don't know if it's pain or medicine or love but I have eyes only for my son. It's not until I hear someone clear their throat that I look up.

The nurse steps forward. "Excuse me, sir, you can't be in here." She puts her hands up toward him to usher him out.

Time stops and his eyes meet mine. He looks at me with pure wonder and I notice he has tears streaming down his cheeks as well.

"Lucas?" Harper says, confused and a little bit horrified. "What are you doing here?"

"It's okay," I croak, and then say it a bit louder. "It's okay."

The nurse turns toward me and then glances back at him suspiciously. He takes a step forward, still not saying anything.

"Rosie, if you want this man to leave just tell me," the nurse says.

I shake my head. "It's okay," I repeat. "He's the father."

45

LUCAS

"WHAT ARE YOU DOING HERE? Is this your idea of a fucking gift basket?"

I hardly hear Harper's voice through the haze in my mind. I had to push past Zach's shocked face outside and I know I might not have a job after this, but it doesn't even matter. All that matters right now is that little baby boy resting on Rosie's chest. The nurse moves closer and I watch her cut the umbilical cord and then swaddle the tiny baby in a cloth.

Harper says something else but I don't hear her. I don't hear anything. All I can see is Rosie and the baby.

"Just a little bit more work to do, and then we'll be all clear," the doctor says. I don't know what he's talking about, but I walk up to the bed as Harper slides out of the way. She looks at me in shock but says nothing as I slip my fingers into Rosie's.

"You look beautiful," I say.

She laughs. "Liar."

The nurse gives Rosie a questioning look and she nods. Before I know what's happening, there's a tiny baby in my arms. He's so light and so small and all of a sudden, I'm terrified of hurting him. I remember how I felt twelve years ago, when Allie was born. That fierce, overwhelming protectiveness washes over me and I look at the little boy, bringing my lips down to his forehead.

My son. I know he's mine.

"Okay, Rosie, just a couple more little pushes, we'll stitch you up and you'll be ready to go. Mr. Dad, you stand out of the way."

The nurses and doctor work quickly to deliver the afterbirth and stitch Rosie up. I stay near her head, and sit down so she can reach over and touch our child.

"I wanted to tell you, Lucas. I just... How... how did you know it was yours?" She asks, her face drawn with worry. I kiss our son's forehead again.

"The timing. I don't know Rosie, I just knew. You'd told me you hadn't slept with anyone."

"And you believed me?"

I frown as I laugh. "Is that a bad thing? Should I not believe you?"

"No, I mean, of course. But wouldn't you feel better getting a paternity test? So you can be sure?"

I look back down at the baby in my arms and am so full of love for him that all I can do is chuckle. "I don't need one, Rosie. I know he's mine. Ours."

I look at her just in time to see her eyes starting to mist up. "Still," she says.

I place the baby back in her arms and she nuzzles her face into the bundle of cloth. Both of us turn toward the door when Allie speaks up.

"I knew it was a boy." She's peering around the corner shyly with a huge grin across her face. Rosie stiffens and I put my hand on her arm.

"Uh, Rosie. This is my daughter, Allie."

Rosie's eyes widen and she looks from me to her. "Allie…"

Allie marches forward and sticks out her hand. "Nice to meet you," she says, shaking Rosie's hand gently. "Congratulations."

"Daughter…" Rosie says, looking from me to Allie.

"I wanted to tell you, but I was afraid you wouldn't be interested in me and then I thought I wouldn't be coming back to New York, and I… I don't know. I'm sorry Rosie."

Allie takes a step forward and looks over toward the baby in Rosie's arms. "He's wrinkly," she announces.

"Allie!" I chide, but Rosie laughs.

"I know. He looks like a tiny old man," she replies, stroking the baby's cheek with a soft, motherly touch. She kisses his forehead and Allie laughs.

"A cute tiny old man. Dad, this is my brother, right?"

My throat tightens. "I, uh, yes. Half-brother."

"Brother," Allie announces. She squints at the little bundle. "I think he looks like me."

I laugh. "I thought he looked like a wrinkly old man?"

Allie shrugs. "He also looks like me."

"Alright kiddo, go wait for me outside. I'll be a couple minutes." Allie scrunches her face but says nothing, instead leaning over and giving Rosie a kiss on the cheek. She turns around and skips out the hospital door and I turn back to Rosie.

"That wasn't the introduction I had in mind," I say. I'm sheepish, hardly daring to look at Rosie.

"Well, this wasn't exactly what I had in mind either," she replies. "What are you doing here?"

"I went to your hospital room and they said you were delivering the baby here."

She laughs. "No, I mean, what are you doing *here*. At the hospital. With me. In New York."

The weight of the question hangs between us. It's hard to swallow as I try to think of something to say.

"I heard you were due and I did the math. I know it's crazy. I didn't even know you were pregnant, Rosie. I would have called."

She shakes her head and the nurse comes to take the baby. "Alright, Dad. It's time to give her some space. We'll get you cleaned up and then back in your room in no time and you guys can talk some more then."

Rosie looks at me and I get up. "I should go see Allie. Do you want anything?"

She shakes her head. "I'll see you back in the hospital room."

All I can do is nod and step outside, closing the door softly behind me and letting all the air out of my lungs. I lean against it with my eyes close and don't move until I hear Harper's voice. I open my eyes to see her standing in front of me, arms crossed with one eyebrow raised.

"Now, Mr. Thorne. Are you going to explain to me why the fuck you thought this was appropriate?"

46

ROSIE

It takes a while for him to latch on, but he gets the hang of it quickly. I watch in amazement as his little mouth works hard to try to extract milk from me.

"This is crazy," I say.

The nurse laughs. "Yep. Don't worry if it takes a day or two for your milk supply to come in. Just breastfeed him as often as possible."

I look up at her and shake my head. "This is crazy," I repeat. "All of it."

She looks at me curiously but says nothing, and I turn back toward the baby. For the next few hours I'm in a daze. I'm wheeled back to my hospital room and fall asleep immediately. When I wake up, Lucas is sitting in the chair next to me reading a magazine. I groan and turn around.

"What time is it?"

He looks at his watch. "6:15 pm."

"Where's the baby?" My heart starts beating faster as my eyes try to adjust to the light in the room.

"Sleeping right there," Lucas answers, pointing to the bassinet next to the bed. I sit back and put my arm over the edge, trailing it over the baby's cheek. I still can't believe how soft his skin is.

"Where're Harper and Jess?"

"They went to get some dinner and I said I'd stay. You want me to call them?"

I shake my head. "No, it's okay." He moves a bit closer and takes my hand in his. He lifts it up and brings it to his lips, kissing my fingers gently. I close my eyes and sigh. Even after it all, even with so many things unsaid between us and a thousand and one questions, it feels good to be near him.

We sit like that, just enjoying each other's company. The baby stirs but doesn't cry. He opens his eyes and blinks at me. Another wave of love crashes over me and I move to pick him up.

"He has blue eyes," I say, bringing him up to my lips for a kiss. "Just like his dad."

Lucas looks from the baby to me and his smile breaks across his face. "Just like his dad," he repeats.

There are so many things I want to tell Lucas, so many things crowding my brain that they all turn to mush and I can't think of anything to say at all. Lucas doesn't seem to mind. He just brings his chair closer and puts his hand behind the baby's head.

"Have you decided on a name yet?"

I shake my head. "Not yet." Lucas's eyes look brighter than I remember. His hair is a bit longer and he has it styled like before, a little bit tousled but still neat. His beard is the same length and his chest is just as broad. His arms pull against the fabric of his shirt as he moves closer to me.

"Lucas," I start. "I've asked the nurses for a paternity test." He looks up at me and frowns.

"Okay," he answers slowly.

"I haven't slept with anyone else," I add quickly. "Not

since I met you. Well, not since months before I met you, really. But I just... I just think considering our history that it would be best."

He nods and I can't tell what he's thinking. He strokes our son's forehead gently and then leans down and kisses my fingers again.

"You don't need to do that," he says.

I shake my head. "I do. Will you take it?"

He nods slowly but says nothing. "If you want me to. But Rosie," he adds. "I know this baby is mine. I watched my daughter be born and I felt the exact same way. This is my son." He pauses. "Our son."

My heart felt full before, but now it's ready to burst. All my fears of Lucas turning his back on me, of him not wanting the kid, of him walking out on me evaporate. He's here. He knows it's his son, he found me and stuck with me as soon as he knew.

A small bloom of hope starts opening up deep inside my chest. Maybe there's a future between us? Maybe there's hope?

I clear my throat. "So, uh," I pause. I don't even know where to start. "What's the plan?"

Lucas laughs. "Don't try to project manage this. There is no plan."

I can't help but smile. "I know there's no plan. I just mean... how long are you here?" My chest tightens as I ask the question. He's brought his young daughter across the country to meet me. Shouldn't she be in school? He left work for the day, he'll have to go back. His whole life is in LA, and my whole life is here. All the problems that were in our way before are still in our way now, except now there's a baby to think about too.

Lucas moves his hand up to my face and strokes my

cheek. "I'll be here as long as it takes to get you settled. I'll have to go to LA to sort things out, and Allie can't miss that much school, but..."

I hang on to every word until he stops talking. "But...?" I repeat.

"But I want to be here for you. Rosie, ever since I met you, I haven't been able to stop thinking about you. I thought you'd walked away from me twice but now I see that you just thought I was using you. This—" he waves his hand between us, "this *thing* that we have, it means something. I want to be with you, Rosie."

I can't even see his face anymore. My eyes are too blurry. The tears drop down my cheeks and I nod.

"I want to be with you, too. I'm sorry, Lucas." My sob interrupts me. "I'm sorry I walked away. I thought..." I can feel my cheeks blushing as the tears stream down it. "I saw a message on your phone and I thought Allie was your wife."

Lucas leans back in his chair, his mouth hanging open and his eyes wide. His lips start curling into a grin and he shakes his head. "You thought you were the *other woman*?"

I nod, unable to get any words out. Lucas starts laughing and shaking his head.

"God, Rosie, if you only knew. There's no one else. There never was anyone else. For the past nine months, ever since I jumped into your taxi, it's been only you."

I laugh as the tears continue to stream out of my eyes.

"I told you it was my taxi," I say, laughing and crying and laughing some more. Before I can say anything else his lips are crushing against mine and his hand is wrapped around the nape of my neck. Our baby stretches and yawns between us and we both smile down at him.

47

LUCAS

It feels wrong to be on the plane back to LA. It feels wrong to leave Rosie and our son behind. It feels wrong to be anywhere except by her side, but I have to go. Allie needs to be in school and I have to somehow explain this to Linda and hand in my resignation.

I haven't laughed or cried this much ever before. My heart feels like it'll explode if any more happiness comes into it.

Allie's sitting beside me, her legs swinging back and forth as she hums to herself.

"I think you should call him Jack," she says.

"Jack? Why Jack?"

"Because of the movie Titanic! Jack and Rose."

I laugh. "Where did you even hear about Titanic? Isn't that a bit inappropriate for you to be watching?"

Allie rolls her eyes. "Everyone knows about Titanic, Dad."

"Right," I respond, elbowing her gently. "I forgot you're all grown up." She grins at me.

"I can't wait to go back. Do they have Mathletes in New York? Where will we live?"

"Whoa, whoa, Allie, slow down. We don't know if we're moving over yet. We don't know what's happening. You're finishing the school year in LA and then we'll see."

Allie's legs stop swinging and she turns toward me. She frowns and shakes her head. "We should be there. They're our family."

Her words cut through me and once again I'm amazed at my twelve year-old daughter's wisdom. Somehow, intuitively, she knows what the right thing to do is.

I mean, I do too. Of course I want to be by Rosie's side. I want to be there for her and for our kid, but there are so many things in the way.

Allie reads my mind. "It's simple, Dad. I finish school this year, you quit your job, we sell the house, and we move. Simple."

I snort. "Doesn't sound simple."

"It is, though. You can go see her every couple of weeks until then and then we get a place in New York."

She does make it sound simple. I shake my head. "You would want to move? What about your friends?"

Allie tilts her head to the side and chews her lip. She nods. "I'll miss them. But I have a little brother now and I need to take care of him. You always tell me that family is the most important."

"That's true, I do say that. And family is the most important thing."

"Right. So that's that." She turns back toward the front of the plane and puts her headphones in, and then turns her head toward me again. "I like Rosie. She's nice."

I shake my head and laugh. She's a little adult, that's for sure. I don't know where she came from but she always succeeds in telling me what the right thing to do is. I'm still not sure it's as simple as she thinks.

. . .

By the time I get back to work, two days after I left, word has traveled about the pregnancy and the trip. Linda is on my heels as I walk into my office.

"Lucas," she says sternly. "What the fuck is going on? When were you going to tell me about this?"

"I didn't even know about it until Jake came back and said she was pregnant."

"You were *fucking* our client this whole time? Do you have any idea what kind of position that puts us in?"

I refrain from making a joke about positions when I see the look on Linda's face. I shrug and then sigh.

"I don't know what to tell you, Linda. We met before we hired Lockwood, before it all happened. I didn't even know she worked there until she walked into the conference room for the proposal. I didn't know!"

Linda shakes her head. "So you're pleading ignorance. You could have told me you had a history. Have you been seeing her this whole time?"

"No. It was over. Well, I thought it was over. I don't know. Listen, Linda. I don't know."

Linda's shoulders relax and she uncrosses her arms. She pulls a chair out and sits across from me. "So, boy or girl?"

"Boy."

A small spark appears in her eye and she starts to smile. "Congratulations."

"Thanks. Listen, Linda, I don't know what is going to happen, but I might need some time off in the next little while."

Linda nods. "Well, that's the other thing I wanted to talk about. After I told you how much I disapprove," she says with the tiniest grin. "I've already spoken to the board about opening up a New York office and proposed you be the director. Hopefully they'll approve it before the gossip reaches them and it won't look like a last-ditch attempt to save face."

My mouth falls open. "I... what?"

"You want to go to New York, don't you? Time off, new baby, beautiful woman there waiting for you...? Isn't that what this is all about?"

My mouth opens and then closes again. What is it with the women in my life knowing what I'm thinking before I've even thought it?

Linda laughs. "Take the day to think about it. I'm waiting on a response from them by the end of the day tomorrow so if you have any objections tell me now." She pauses and leans forward slightly. "You've been a great employee and a great friend, Lucas. When your wife died, something in you changed. You got so serious, and you worked harder than anyone in their right mind should work."

I swallow and try to say something but she holds up her hand. "For a few months I saw that spark in you again, and when I heard about the baby it all made sense. Be with your family. Be with the woman you love."

"I don't—"

Linda holds up her hand. "Whatever you're about to say, don't say it. Think about the New York office and let me know by tomorrow morning."

I nod and she turns around and walks out the door. I sit back in my chair and stare at the open doorway in awe. Somehow, Linda has managed to solve a dozen of my problems without even asking. Her words play in my head on repeat: *Be with your family. Be with the woman you love.*

The woman you love.

I sigh and shake my head before pulling out my phone.

Rosie answers right away. "Hello?"

"You'll never guess what just happened," I say as the smile starts to spread from my face down through my heart.

48

ROSIE

I THINK I've had seventeen minutes of sleep in the past four days. That's what it feels like, anyway. Lucas just texted me, he's on his way from the airport. I look down at myself and sigh. I'm wearing an old tee-shirt I got for free at a fundraiser event, and my grey sweatpants have stains all over the front. I'm not sure I own anything that doesn't have stains all over the front anymore.

Jack is asleep in his crib so I rush to the bathroom. I wash in the sink and pull a brush through my hair before swiping mascara over my lashes and putting a bit of blush on. I put on a bra and wince before changing my mind. I slip on a light summer dress and a cardigan just as the apartment buzzer rings.

He's here.

When I open the door, my heart does a full backflip. My stomach twists into knots and my mouth goes dry. I lick my lips and smile.

"Hi."

"Hi," he says, staring back at me. We stand and look at

each other as I try to take in every detail of his face. He clears his throat. "Can I come in?"

"Oh! Right. Yes. Obviously."

I step aside and he comes in rolling a small suitcase behind him. He smells just like I remember and suddenly I feel that warmth spreading in my center. The doctor said no sex for four to six weeks, and it's hardly even been one. I'm not sure I'll be able to handle that.

Lucas puts his suitcase to the side and turns around as I close the door. He takes a step toward me and wraps his arms around me. I melt into his warmth, groaning in satisfaction as my cheek hits his chest and his hands travel up and down my spine.

"You look beautiful," he breathes. "Radiant."

I laugh. "Thanks."

Just then, Jack wakes up and starts wailing. His cries are high-pitched and piercing and I'm learning to tell them apart.

"He's hungry," I explain. "Welcome to my life," I call out over my shoulder as I head toward the crib.

Lucas appears beside me and puts a hand on the small of my back as I pick the baby up. "Our life," he corrects. "I'm here."

Somehow, those two little words mean more than just 'I'm here.' They fill me with a sense of deep comfort and stability, and make my heart beat a little bit harder. He stays next to me as I coax Jack to take my breast and start nursing. Lucas lays a gentle kiss on my head and sighs.

"Have I ever told you how much I love your hair? It's like fire," he says, kissing my head again.

"If you start calling me firecrotch I'm kicking you out," I laugh, poking him in the ribs. He chuckles and wraps his arms around my shoulder a little bit tighter and I rest my head on his chest. It feels so nice to be in his arms, like I'm finally home.

Jack finishes nursing and I put him up on my shoulder to burp him. Once that's done, he falls asleep right away and I set him down in his crib. Lucas strokes his cheek with a finger. My heart flips in my chest as I watch him look at our son, and the heat of desire starts blossoming inside me. I slip my fingers into Lucas's and he turns toward me, wrapping me in his arms once again. We melt together and he traces the line of my jaw before dipping his lips toward mine.

This kiss feels different. Every time we've seen each other, there's been a fierceness to our desire. Our bodies just tore at each other and we couldn't get close enough. Now, he brings his lips to mine and brushes them against me ever so softly. We kiss gently, tenderly, like nothing exists except the two of us.

My skin feels so sensitive, and every time he touches me, I feel little currents flow through me. I press myself against him and can feel every thread of clothing that he wears. His fingers cup my cheek and then tangle into my hair and I melt into him more, the two of us slowly, gently, melting together until our bodies and entangled.

He pulls away and puts his hands on either side of my face, tilting it up toward him. His eyes are still a deep blue, but they're not piercing. The softness in them makes me shiver and I feel happiness blossom deep inside my chest.

"I want you," I whisper. "I wish my vagina wasn't out of commission."

Lucas chuckles. "Relax yourself," he says as he strokes my hair. "We have all the time in the world. Let's just get to know each other and get to know Jack and enjoy this. I'm here now."

Those words again—*I'm here*—go straight through my

heart. My knees start trembling and I press myself against his chest. Jack gurgles and wriggles in his crib beside us and we look over at the tiny human beside us. Lucas holds me tighter and brushes his lips against my forehead. I close my eyes and lean into him and let the happiness engulf me.

49

LUCAS

THERE ARE SO many things to say, but we say nothing. She's in bed beside me, trailing her fingers over and back across my chest as I groan in contentment. My cock pulses. The feeling of having her here beside me, knowing she's mine, knowing we're together, it's almost too much.

Rosie can feel it too. She trails her hand down toward my crotch and my desire intensifies. I catch her hand before she touches me.

"It's okay, Rosie. I want to wait until we can do things together. I want you to feel as good as me," I whisper, turning my head to look at her eyes.

Rosie smiles. "How do you know it doesn't make me feel good to do things to you? You can't expect me to lie here and not want to touch you."

Every word makes my cock more sensitive. It's harder than it was a minute ago and I know if she keeps running her fingers over my chest and stomach it'll get harder still. I move my arm out of the way and her fingers walk down my stomach, circle around my belly button and finally grab my cock.

She wraps her fingers around my cock and my whole

body shivers. A groan escapes my lips and my cock pulses in her palm. She chuckles softly and moans before stroking me, softly at first, and then faster and faster.

I didn't know it could feel this good to have a woman's hand around my shaft. I always thought I could do it better myself, but I was wrong. There's no comparison. She moves her hand up and down and presses her body against mine and before I know it, my balls are tightening up toward my body.

"I'm going to come," I pant. "You're going to make me come."

"So come," Rosie whispers. Her voice is seductive and with those two words my whole body contracts. It feels like red hot blood flowing out from my center to every extremity of my body. I moan and throw my head back as Rosie keeps stroking me until I'm completely empty.

Panting, I open my eyes and turn my head toward Rosie.

"Whoa," I say. She's not looking at me, she moving her hand up from my cock to my stomach. She trails her fingers through my seed and laughs.

"Messy," she says.

"I'm destroyed," I respond. "Fuck."

She laughs again and the sound is almost as good as my orgasm. I groan and get up, shuffling to the bathroom to clean up. I poke my head out the door and look back at her.

"That was hot."

She laughs again and nods. "Yep. I'll be keeping that one in the old spank bank for sure."

"Spank bank?" I arch an eyebrow, turning back to the sink.

"I have needs, you know," she laughs. In a few seconds I'm climbing back into bed beside her and wrapping my arms around her.

"I'll be taking care of your needs the second the doctor says it's okay." I say, burying my face in her curls. She holds me tighter.

"You're already taking care of my needs."

"Rosie," I say gently.

She nuzzles her head into my shoulder. "Mm-hmm."

"I'm going to start looking for a place to stay. Somewhere big enough for the four of us. What do you think?"

She stiffens slightly and looks up at me. "The four of us. Like, you and me, Jack and Allie?"

I nod. "Somewhere where we can be together."

Rosie gulps and lays back, staring at the ceiling. "I've been in this apartment for years," she says slowly. "I guess I hadn't thought about it. Not right now. I assumed I'd stay here until I can afford to move."

I roll onto my side and brush her hair away from her face. She turns her head toward me and her face is lined with worry.

"Sorry," she says, trying to smile. "It's just moving so fast. All of a sudden I have not only one kid but two and also a boyfriend."

"I get it. Just think about it. I can find somewhere for Allie and me in the meantime and you can keep your place."

Rosie nods and relaxes. "Okay." She smiles for real this time and wraps her arms around me again. "Thank you for understanding."

All I do is squeeze her against me and stroke her skin with my fingers. Slowly, I can feel her relaxing and starting to trust me.

She pulls her head back and looks at me. "I have something," she says slowly. "While we're talking about important things."

"Get it out of the way, quick, or else we'll be back to saying nothing to each other," I laugh. She smiles and gets up, opening a drawer in her dresser. She pulls out a white envelope and sits down on the bed beside me. Her legs are crossed and she stares at the envelope in her hand before turning it around for me to see.

"Lab results. From the paternity test."

A lump forms in my throat and I nod. As much as I tell myself the baby is mine, and I know in my heart it's mine, that little piece of paper could change things. It wouldn't change anything for me, I am still exactly where I want to be, but it might change things for her.

Rosie's hands are shaking and she brings her palm to her forehead before sticking the envelope toward me. She shakes her head.

"I can't do it."

I take it out of her hands and sit up, wrapping my arms around her.

"Rosie, listen to me," I say, pulling away and running the back of my finger down her cheek. "That baby is mine, no matter what the paper says. I'm moving to New York with Allie to set up the new office and most importantly to be with you and Jack. I don't need some scientist to tell me that's my son."

Tears stream down her face and she nods.

"Open it," Rosie croaks.

Now my hands are shaking. I tear the envelope open and pull the single sheet of paper out. My eyes start blurring as the tears well up in my eyes. I can hardly scan the rest of the paper. All I see are the numbers 99.98% match.

"He's our son, Rosie."

She makes yelp and throws her hands around me. Her body starts shaking with sobs as she cries on my shoulder. I rub my hands down her back and rock back and forth until she sits back.

"This is so silly," she laughs. "You're the only person I've had sex with in over a year but I was still worried."

"Stop worrying," I say gently. "I told you I'm here, and I mean it."

THE NEXT FEW weeks pass in a flash. I spend a few days in New York, seeing Rosie and Jack and setting up the new office. Then, I go back to LA to be with Allie and make sure things are going well with work. This happens over and over again as I move back and forth. It's hectic, and before I know it, Allie's school year is just about finished.

"So I'll land tomorrow morning but I have to go straight to work," I say over the phone. "I'll come over as soon as I'm done. Should be about noon or so." Rosie makes a noise and then I hear Jack in the background, wailing his head off.

"Sounds good. I have to go."

I get that familiar feeling before I'm about to see Rosie. It's probably what people mean when they say butterflies in the stomach. My bag is already packed and I find Allie and my mother in the living room.

"Okay Allie, one more trip and then we'll head over together. Thanks for taking care of her mom."

"No problem, sweetie. I'll be sad to see you two go. When did you say I could come meet the new baby?"

"Let us get settled first, Mom."

My mother purses her lips but she nods. I know it's killing her to be away from her new grandson, but she'll have to wait until Rosie and I move in together—whenever Rosie's ready to do it. The two of them give me a hug and a kiss and I leave to fly across the country one more time.

50

ROSIE

JACK IS SLEEPING for longer and longer stretches, and I'm starting to feel human again. I fix my hair and put makeup on as I wait for Lucas to get here. I adjust the black lacy lingerie I'm wearing and take a deep breath. He should be here any minute and my heart is thumping. It's been five weeks, and the doctor said I was good to go.

We've had sex plenty of times before, and he's the father of my child, but somehow this time I'm more nervous. We've spent time together and started raising our son together now, so it feels a lot more intimate. Somehow it feels more real than when we first met.

The buzzer sounds and I jump. He's here.

My heart is pounding against my ribcage as I head toward the door. I buzz him upstairs and check my outfit one last time. I'm wearing a matching black bra and thong, and slipped a satin dressing gown over my shoulders. Why am I so nervous? He's seen me naked plenty of times. He's kissed every inch of my body, both pre- and post-baby. I look down at the little baby pouch on my stomach and purse my lips, and then shake my head and think of the way he's held me and stroked me for the past few weeks.

The knock on the door makes me jump again and I take a deep breath. With one hand on the doorknob and another smoothing my hair one last time, I swing the door open.

"Hey—"

His jaw drops. He scans my body up and down for a second, mouth agape and eyes bulging out of his head. My cheeks start to burn up and I shift my weight from one foot to the other.

"Hey," I say softly. "You like it?"

My voice seems to shake him out of his stupor. He flicks his eyes up to mine. "Like it? Yes. Yes, I like it. The doctor...?"

"Ready to go," I answer with both thumbs up. A grin spreads across his face.

With that, he steps inside and slams the door closed behind him. His arms are around my body and he lifts me up, holding me close. I wrap my legs around his waist and crush my lips against his. His fingers find the nape of my neck and the passion between us erupts. My arms are around his neck, running through his hair and down his spine. My tongue is brushing against his lips, diving into his mouth and feeling his tongue against it. His hands are on my neck, my back, my ass as he walks toward the sofa.

He lays me down gently and pulls away. I laugh.

"Just like the first time," I say, nodding toward the couch.

He grins. "Hopefully we won't have any surprises this time."

"I'm on the pill now."

Without a word, he dips his head toward me. His lips brush against my neck, nibble my earlobe and kiss my jaw. He tastes my lips again before trailing kisses all the way down toward my chest.

"I like this," he says, running his fingers over my bra. "It's nice."

"Thanks," I respond as I start grinding my hips toward him. He groans. His fingers trace the line of my bra over my breasts and he kisses the soft skin on my chest.

Just like the first time we met, he touches every scar on my body with his fingers and follows with kiss after kiss. He takes his time, kissing my skin over and over until every scar has been covered, and then he moves over my stomach and kisses it as well.

"I love your body," he breathes. All I can do is moan in response. The way he touches me is electric. His hands send sparks flying off my skin as he explores my body like the first time. His mouth kisses every little bit of skin it encounters and he groans with pleasure. I buck my hips up toward him and reach down between us.

"You're so hard," I breathe. He chuckles softly and keeps kissing the skin on my stomach. His hand travels from my knee up my thigh and his fingers dig into the flesh near my hip. I tilt them toward him and he hooks his fingers into my panties. He kisses the hem of my underwear softly, staring at the black against my pale skin.

When he slides my underwear off, he does it slowly. He trails kisses all the way down my legs as he peels the fabric off my body. His hands travel all the way back up my legs and he massages the tops of my thighs with his hands. His thumbs graze against my slit and I shiver.

"I want you," I breathe. "I want you so bad."

He grins at me, still moving his hands in slow, long movements. Every time he brushes his fingers closer and closer to my slit it makes me quiver and moan.

"Stop teasing me," I breathe, and again all he does is grin and tease. I reach up toward his waistband and he pulls his shirt off. My hands roam over every smooth muscle as they ripple under his skin. He pulls his pants off and his cock springs free. I gasp, and he chuckles.

"It missed you," he says, stroking his cock gently.

"I missed it too," I say, biting my lip and watching his hand move back and forth. With his other hand he drags a finger along my slit and moans.

"So wet," he whispers. Before I can respond, he's plunging his cock inside me from the tip to the hilt. It fills me up completely until nothing exists except him, me, and the pleasure exploding in my body. The pressure builds in my core as my hands claw at his skin, pushing him to thrust deeper and deeper inside me. He grunts and moans, glistening with a thin film of sweat as our bodies stay locked together.

It's more than sex this time. It's more than attraction or lust. It's more than whatever was pulling us toward each other all those months ago.

This is the father of my child. His movements are my movements. His moans are my moans. His body is my body and we move together until I don't know where he ends and I begin. He pushes himself deeper inside me and my back arches. I open my eyes and gasp as he enters me again and again.

Our eyes meet and a grin spreads on his lips.

"I love you, Rosie," he pants. "I love you so much."

Without warning, my orgasm erupts. The instant his words reach my ears, my body contracts and pleasure races through my veins until all I can see is him and all I can feel is his body around me, against me, inside me.

I try to answer but all that comes out are gasps and noises until I close my eyes and let the pleasure transport me out of my mind and out of my body.

My body contracts around him and I let it go. I let it all go.

The air leaves my lungs and the thoughts leave my head as he thrusts himself into me just a little bit deeper.

I feel his cock get harder and start pulsing and I know he's coming. I open my eyes to see his mouth form that satisfied 'o' and I smile, gasping for air.

"I love you, too," I answer. "I love you, too."

Those words mean more to me than I can imagine. Our bodies are locked together, our legs entangled and our arms wrapped around each other. We let our orgasms subside and then recover slowly, heartbeats slowing down together and breath mixing as the life comes back to our bodies.

Lucas leans against his elbow and strokes my face, tucking a strand of hair behind my ear.

"I love you," he says again. "I don't want to stop saying it. I love you, Rosie."

My smile feels like it's splitting my face from ear to ear. My eyes are misting up and I blink away the happiest tears I've ever had.

"I love you too, Lucas." I take a deep breath, gazing up into his eyes. "I think I'm ready to move in together, too."

Lucas's face breaks into a smile. The father of my child, the father of my children leans down and brushes his lips against mine. He's here, and I'm here, and we have two healthy, happy children. I didn't know one person could be so lucky, and I definitely didn't think that person could be me. I can't help it. I have to say those three magical words again:

"I love you."

EPILOGUE

ROSIE

"SHE'S GOING TO LOVE YOU," Lucas says, placing a kiss on my forehead. "Don't worry."

"Okay," I answer. "It's just been a long time since I've had to meet the parents."

"My mother is more concerned with meeting Jack and spoiling him rotten than anything else," he answers, laughing. "You'll be lucky if she even notices you."

I turn back toward the arrivals gate and take another breath. His mother should be walking through any minute, and I bounce Jack in my arms. Allie jumps up and down beside me.

"Do you think Grandma brought any of her gingersnap cookies?" She turns to me. "They're my favorite. We used to make them together all the time."

"If she didn't bring any, I'm sure you'll have time to make some together," I respond. Two whole weeks to make them.

I'll welcome the help with Jack, but I'm still nervous. Two weeks with the mother-in-law. Not technically, obviously, but she's my mother-in-law for all intents and purposes. She's said that she wants to help with the baby in any way possible, but I've heard so many horror stories about mothers-in-law that I'm not sure what to think.

When she steps through the sliding doors, I know it's her before Lucas says anything. She has his eyes, and his smile. She spots him and smiles immediately, then her eyes travel to Allie and then to me and the baby. Allie starts running toward her and Lucas's mother spreads her arms wide. I can't help but smile as Allie collides with her grandmother, who wraps her in an embrace that only grandmas can give.

"Grandma!" Allie squeals, pulling away and slipping her hand into the old woman's. She greets Lucas with a warm hug and a kiss on the cheek and then turns to me.

"And you must be Rosie. It's a pleasure to meet you, I'm Martha."

"Hi Martha, this is Jack. Lucas tells me you've been wanting to meet him for some time now."

Martha's face crinkles as she sees Jack. She opens her arms and I pass him over. My heart melts as I see the wonder on her face. She brings him up to her face and kisses his forehead.

"He's beautiful," she breathes. "What a beautiful boy."

"Thank you," I reply, glancing at Lucas. He winks at me and then turns to his mother.

"Do you have all your bags? We should get going."

"Oh, you're always rushing, rushing, rushing," Martha chides. "I've only just met my grandson!"

"Come on, Mom," Lucas laughs. "You can spoil him when we get to the house."

All my fears about the next two weeks evaporate. Martha is warm and friendly, and I can tell she has nothing but love for Lucas, Allie, and Jack. Maybe even a little bit for me. It's a flurry of activity as we get her moved into the guest room and get Allie to bed. Finally, I get to sit down in the living room with Jack in my arms. Martha and Lucas come and join me.

"Thank you for having me, it's very kind of you," Martha says.

"Oh please, of course we'd have you. We just needed to move into the new place before there was enough room. My old apartment was a typical New York shoebox," I laugh.

Lucas nods. "It was small." His eyes gleam, and I know he's happy that we've finally moved in together. I loved that he gave me space, but it didn't take me long to realize I couldn't live without him.

Martha glances at me and I nod to Jack. "You want to hold him? He's sleeping but I think he's taken a liking to you already."

Martha beams and holds out her arms. I watch as she rocks him back and forth and takes in all his tiny features. Lucas and I exchange a glance and he smiles. I shake my head, not believing how lucky I've been. A year ago I was recovering from the traumatic stabbing by Harper's stalker, and now I've inherited the most loving family I could imagine.

Martha looks at me and then at Lucas. She nods to the baby and I take Jack back, and then she glances at her hands. She pulls off the ring on her left hand and holds it to Lucas.

"Now, I know I should wait to do this, but I can just sense the love you have for each other and for that baby and the little girl upstairs. I always knew you'd find someone," she starts.

"Mom," Lucas interjects, but stops when she shoots him a glance.

Martha continues: "This was my mother's ring." She holds it up to Lucas. "Now you don't need to give it to her right now, but I want you to have it. This is a special woman and a special ring. Since your father died, I haven't needed it. It should be worn by someone younger than me."

"Mom, I..." Lucas starts again. There's a lump in my throat and all I can do is watch. Martha shakes her head and hands the ring to Lucas, who takes it gently. He holds it up to his face and inspects it for a few moments before looking at me.

"Well," he says, and then stands up and kneels down in front of me. "No sense in waiting. Rosie, I love you more than anyone or anything else in this whole world. You're the mother of my child, and you've become a mother to Allie ever since you met her. I can't imagine my life without you." I can see the tears in his eyes as mine mist up. I still can't say anything from the lump in my throat.

Lucas stares deep in my eyes. "Marry me, Rosie."

The smile cracks my face open. I don't know if I've ever smiled this hard, or this sincerely in my whole life. I nod. "Yes," I whisper, and then say a bit louder. "*Yes.*"

Lucas laughs and slips the ring over my finger. He puts his hands on either side of my face and kisses me harder than ever before. We're both shaking, and I can't stop smiling and laughing as we pull away.

"Yay!" Allie's voice calls out from the top of the stairs.

"You're supposed to be in bed," Lucas yells. Allie runs downstairs and jumps up. I'm laughing and smiling so hard my cheeks hurt.

"Well, that's settled then," Martha says, sitting back. "Now let me see my grandson again."

I laugh again and nod, handing Jack over to his doting grandmother.

"Lucky kid," I breathe. I look at Lucas and Allie and Martha. "Lucky me."

∼

Keep reading for a preview of **Book 3: Knocked Up Again**

Don't forget to grab your FREE bonus extended epilogue by signing up to my reader list:

https://www.lilianmonroe.com/subscribe

If you're already signed up, you can follow the link in your welcome email to access the bonus content from all my books.

xox Lilian

KNOCKED UP... AGAIN!

KNOCKED UP: BOOK 3

1

JESS

My grandmother's old house hasn't changed a bit. Well, the paint is peeling a little and it's faded over the years. There are a few more weeds in the flower beds but apart from that, it looks exactly the same.

I park the car and grab my bag. I packed light—there's no one to impress in this town. In any case, Gram will probably want to stuff me so full of food I'll need a new wardrobe by the time my ten day trip is over.

My steps are light as I make my way up the flagstone path toward the wide front porch. I remember playing on the path, skipping from flagstone to flagstone when I was a kid, over and back for hours at a time. I grin as I place my feet on the stones and avoid the bits of grass that stick up between them. Old habits die hard, I guess.

By the time I make it to the porch and put my foot on the first rickety step, the screen door swings open.

"Jessica," my grandmother's warm voice greets me. Her wrinkled face is lit up with a huge smile, and she steps out to spread her arms wide.

"Hi, Gram." I hop up the steps and drop my bag before

wrapping my grandmother in a huge bear hug. "It's good to see you."

She smiles at me and strokes my cheek with a gnarled finger. "Good to see you too, darling. Come on in. Is that all you brought?"

"Just the one bag."

She nods and her eyebrow shoots up. "Well all right. Your old room is all made up. You put your things down and come to the kitchen for some food."

She gives my arm a squeeze and flashes me another smile and then disappears down the hallway toward the kitchen. I take a few moments to glance around and smile. Nothing's changed. To the right is the living room with the old over-stuffed sofa that we weren't allowed to sit on when we were kids. Straight ahead is the creaky stairway up to the bedrooms with the white handrail curling around at the bottom in a graceful arc. I run my fingers along the wain-scoting at waist height and take in the old paisley wallpaper that must be older than I am.

I'm home.

My room hasn't changed at all. From the time I moved in when I was seven to the time I moved out when I was eigh-teen, this was my refuge. The small single bed with the floral bedspread is still in the corner, and my favorite teddy bear is carefully placed in front of the pillows. I drop my bag and pick the faded brown bear up.

"Hey, Mr. Tickles. How have you been?"

Mr. Tickles looks back at me with his glassy eyes and I bring him up to my nose. I breathe in deeply and sigh. I spent hours hugging that bear until I fell asleep when I was a little girl. I put him back down on the bed and scan the room. My medals from sports, the trophy I won in a debate tournament, the certificates of achievement for schoolwork—it's all displayed exactly how I had it when I was here. I shake my head. Gram must have thought I was going to move back in eventually.

THERE WASN'T a hope on Earth that I'd move back in. Lexington, Virginia isn't exactly the belly button of the universe, and it certainly wasn't the most pleasant place for me to grow up. Apart from Gram who loved me unconditionally, I was always an outsider here. I got out as soon as that college acceptance letter came through.

The stairs creak as I make my way back to the kitchen. I step through the door and let it swing back and forth behind me. Gram looks over her shoulder.

"Come here, dear. I've made some chicken for you. Grab a plate."

"Smells delicious, Gram."

"Just simple cooking," she responds as she spoons the fragrant meat onto my plate. "You look as thin as a rail, Jessica. Eat up."

I laugh and shake my head. "You're always trying to fatten me up, Gram."

"You young people need food. It's good for you."

I grab a knife and fork and sit down at the kitchen table. Gram keeps working away, stirring and cleaning and hustling and bustling around the kitchen. I take my first bite and groan.

"This is so good," I say.

"Do they not have chicken in New York?"

"They have chicken," I laugh, "but not your chicken."

"Mm." That's all the response I get as Gram looks over to make sure I'm eating my fill. It would be hard not to, I haven't had anything this tasty in months.

"So what's new in town? There must be some news?"

"Oh, not much. Old Mr. Wilson died, and Mrs. Wilson looks like she's on the way out. Jack Hanson's daughter is getting married to a boy from Clivestown. Melanie Sanders just had a baby boy, the most precious little baby you've ever seen."

"Deaths, weddings and babies, huh," I reply as I take another bite.

"That's life, Jessica," Gram responds as she finally pulls out a chair to sit down. "How about you? When am I going to meet the lucky man who snagged you?"

I laugh. "No one's been that lucky, Gram. You know I'd tell you if I was seeing someone. I think I'm destined to be an old maid."

"Nonsense. You're smart and beautiful and kind. Surely there's someone in that big city that means something to you?"

"Not yet," I laugh. "Not a man, anyways. I'm not in any rush to get married Gram. And you know me, I'm not interested in having kids."

Gram makes a noise and nods her head. "You might change your mind when the right man comes along," she says with a smile.

I shake my head. "Doubt it. I'm not bringing a kid into this world, it's too miserable. I wouldn't do that to an innocent child."

This time, Gram's face crinkles up and she starts laughing. "It's always been doom and gloom with you, Jessica. You haven't changed a bit."

"I prefer to call it realism," I reply as I scrape my plate for the last bits of sauce. I glance at my grandmother and smile. She takes my plate. "I'll get that, Gram. Let me do something to help."

"Don't worry about it, dear. You go see your friends. I know Samantha is dying to see you."

"I was thinking you and I would hang out tonight, Gram. I haven't seen you in so long."

Gram smiles and plants a kiss on my cheek. "You should go out and enjoy yourself. It's Friday night! There's a new owner at the Lexington Hotel. He's having some big dinner or concert or party over there tonight. Lots of young people and such. You should go. The new owner is some big shot from New York, maybe you know him."

A party at the Lex. Great.

I snort. "Doubt it. It's a bit bigger than this town, Gram. What happened to Mrs. Carter? Why did she sell the hotel?"

"When Hank died, I think a part of her died with him and she just wanted to get rid of the place," Gram replies. "That's how it goes with us old folks. Me too, but I'm just too stubborn to die," she adds with a smile.

"You're not dying anytime soon, Gram."

"Mm-hmm. Now go. The whole town will be there, you'll see everyone."

"Get all the hellos out of the way tonight, then I can just lay low for the rest of the week."

Gram laughs. "Go, my little social butterfly." She wraps me in one of her hugs again and plants a big kiss on my cheek. "It's good to see you, Jessica."

"It's good to see you too, Gram. I missed you."

"Go and have fun. I'll see you in the morning." Her eyes crinkle as she smiles at me and I wrap my arms around her in another hug. Even if Lexington never felt like home, my grandmother's arms always did.

2

JESS

IT's nice to be back in the warm weather. There's quite a bit of a nip in the air, but that's to be expected at the end of April. New York is still freezing cold this time of year so this feels almost balmy. I wrap my jacket around me a little bit tighter and walk down toward Main Street.

The streets are so quiet here. Compared to the big city where everyone is in a rush and there's constant noise of cars and honking and yelling, it's almost shocking to be somewhere like this. It feels like a different universe. I glance up at the sky and see the first stars start to twinkle as dusk falls.

I take a deep breath and let the clean air fill my lungs as I turn onto Main Street. When I exhale, I can see my breath for a second before it dissipates and I take a couple deep breaths just to watch them disappear.

The hotel comes into view just down the road—it must be absolutely packed. Every man and their dog are probably there. The new owner has put lights up on all the eaves and painted the whole thing. It looks like there's a new sign, too. I speed up slightly, curious to see what else has changed.

As I get closer, the noise gets louder. It sounds like live

music and the whole town talking and shouting and singing. There's a huge banner over the front door: *Grand Re-Opening.*

Very grand, I think with a grin. I don't think the Lex could be described as 'Grand' even if the Queen of England decided to buy it.

"Well, if it isn't Jessica Lee," comes a voice to the left and a chill goes down my spine. It's the voice that bullied me all throughout high school for being a nerd, or a tomboy, or whatever it was that made me not fit in here. Miss Popularity.

"Mary Hanson," I reply. "I heard you're getting married. Congratulations." My voice sounds flat even to my ears.

"Thank you," she says, extending her hand and wiggling her fingers at me. The huge rock on her finger glimmers in the light and I nod.

"Nice ring."

"Oh, thank you," she replies, pulling her hand back and admiring the ring on her perfectly manicured hand. "He did well."

"Mm," I say, glancing around for a way to extract myself from the conversation. "Who's the lucky guy?"

"He's a gem," she replies as she flicks her long blonde hair over her shoulder and giggles. "No pun intended."

Either that or he's gotten a lobotomy and doesn't realize what he's getting himself into.

"How about you?" She asks innocently. "Any wedding bells or are you still all *alone*?"

I bristle. "Living the single life in the big city," I reply. "Tinder's number 1 user."

Mary purses her lips and nods. "Well you haven't changed a bit."

I say nothing, trying to ignore the thinly veiled insult. I paint a smile on my face as the anger starts to swell in my chest. She flicks her hair behind her shoulder and smirks.

"How long are you in town for?" She finally asks to break the silence. She doesn't try to conceal the look of disdain as her eyes scan me from head to toe. A small part of me wishes I was wearing something nicer than jeans, a tank top and a plain jacket and I hate myself for thinking it.

"Ten days," I reply. "Visiting Gram for Easter."

"Well you *have* to come by for dinner one night. I have *so much* to tell you."

"I'm sure you do. Sounds good, I'll see you then!" I turn to the hotel entrance and slip inside before she can make any real plans with me. Dinner with Mary Hanson and the poor soul who's marrying her sounds like my idea of Hell.

The noise inside the hotel is loud. There's a band on stage and people dancing like maniacs. The bar is packed with familiar faces and the whole place is decorated in balloons, garlands, and little lights on all the rafters.

My eyes scan the room and a smile starts forming on my lips. I shake my shoulders and try to forget about Mary Hanson.

She disappears from my head completely when someone steps beside me. I smell his cologne before anything else. It smells almost spicy, but with a surprising freshness. Like a magnet pulling my head, I turn to see the most incredible looking man I've ever seen in my life. I think he stepped out of GQ Magazine and into the Lexington Hotel by accident. My body tenses immediately and I can't see anything but him.

He's staring at me with eyes the color of mahogany. His lips are plump and perfect, and there's a hint of stubble over his strong jaw. His hair is dark brown and styled effortlessly.

"Do I know you?" He asks, tilting his head slightly and then licking his lips.

His words almost don't register, because I'm too busy

staring at his lips. They move just a bit when he speaks, and then spread into a small smile. His voice is as smooth as butter and it pierces through my chest and sends a thrill straight through my stomach.

I clear my throat. "Uh, no. No, I don't think so."

"I'm Owen," he says and his voice almost makes me fall over. He raises his hand toward me and on autopilot, I slip mine into it.

"Jessica," I reply. It comes out as a croak just as our palms touch. Another thrill goes down my spine and I inhale sharply. His hand is warm and wide and it covers my palm completely. His hands feel... not rough, exactly, but solid. We stay like that for a second that lasts an eternity until he smiles again.

"Enjoy your evening, Jessica."

"Call me Jess. I will. Thanks. You too."

"Jess," he replies as if he's tasting my name in his mouth. My whole body buzzes as my name leaves his lips.

His fingers slip away and he looks at me one last time before turning and weaving his way through the crowd. He's a good six inches taller than most people, and as wide as a football player, but he slides through the crowd almost gracefully. It's like they part around him like a school of fish around a shark without even noticing what they're doing.

I'm pulled out of my daze by another voice.

"Jess! You met our sexy new mystery owner!" I smile and turn to see the familiar freckled face of my oldest and kindest friend.

"I guess I did. How are you, Sam?"

She wraps me in a hug and laughs. "It's great to see you. You look amazing!"

It's my turn to laugh. "Doubt it, but thanks. Come on, let

me buy you a drink and you can tell me everything I've missed."

She snorts. "That'll be a quick conversation. You haven't missed a thing."

I laugh as we turn to the bar, and I can't help glancing back toward the place in the crowd where Owen disappeared. My hand tingles where he touched it as I turn back to Sam and smile. She's right about one thing, he's definitely mysterious, and undeniably sexy.

3
___

OWEN

I NEVER THOUGHT MOVING to a small town would be easy but I didn't think it would be this hard. It's possible that New Yorkers might actually be more welcoming than this place. When I first arrived, news had travelled far that there was a new owner of the Lexington Hotel and I got the immediate sense that there were lots of people that weren't too happy about it.

Even tonight, with the whole town out to celebrate the grand re-opening, I see a lot of sideways glances.

I've heard a lot of the rumors about me. I'm some billionaire, running away from a sordid past. They say my wife left me, or she died, or I killed her. They say I don't have a wife, and that the loneliness drove me to leave New York. They say I stole my money and now I need someplace to bury it so the IRS doesn't come after me.

They say I coerced Gladys Carter into selling the hotel, but the truth is she approached my real estate agent. She was desperate to sell, and I saw an opportunity.

That's what I do.

I take opportunities and I make them work. That's how I

made my money. That's why I left New York. That's why I'll leave this place as soon as I see another opportunity.

I'm not some dark, mysterious billionaire out to swindle kind townsfolk. I'm just a guy with a pocketful of cash and a particular skill at turning that into more cash. That's my story whenever anyone asks, anyways.

Sure, I've got skeletons in my closet, but who doesn't? Whatever was going on in New York is behind me now.

That blonde woman walks back into the hotel and our eyes meet for a brief second—what's her name again? Mary something? She raises her hands and wiggles her fingers at me while batting her eyelashes. I dip my chin down slightly. For a woman that's about to get married, she sure does throw a lot of glances around the room.

I turn away from her and pray that she doesn't come toward me. I lean against one of the old timber pillars that line the outside of the room and run my fingers through my hair. The townspeople love to gossip, but they certainly didn't refuse an invitation. There are people everywhere dancing, talking, drinking, shouting. You might even call tonight a success. My eyes scan the bar for the other woman, the one I've never seen before.

Jess.

That's one name I won't forget. There she is. She's at the bar with another girl, the friendly freckle-faced girl that helped me when I got a flat tire last week. They're laughing. Jess throws her head back and her whole body doubles over as she laughs at something the other girl said. She wipes a tear from her eye and I lean forward, as if I'd be able to hear what they're saying from over here.

Then, she lifts her eyes as if they were drawn to me. I can see that spark in them that I saw earlier. There's a hint of a smile on her lips and all of a sudden, it's just me and her. I can't hear the band. I can't see a single other person, or hear the shouting of two hundred voices. It's just me and her, eyes locked on each other from opposite ends of the room.

It feels like we're on a moving train, and everything and everyone in the room is whipping past at a hundred miles an hour except for her. I can almost smell that floral perfume she was wearing.

Then, she turns her head to her friend and I'm rocked back into the real world. My heart's racing and I blink three or four times. I realize I'm holding a bottle of beer and I bring the cold liquid to my lips.

What just happened?

I need to find out who she is.

I can't help myself. My eyes swing back to her. One of the young guys from town is walking up to her and she greets him warmly. She opens her arms and they hug for what seems like an eternity. Jealousy starts curdling in my stomach as I watch them pull apart, and then she runs her hands over his arms. Everyone laughs and I wish I knew what it was about.

They stop touching each other and my shoulders immediately relax. I turn away from them and take another angry sip of beer.

What the fuck is wrong with me?

I don't know this woman! I just learned her name three minutes ago. And now I'm jealous that she gave some guy a hug? She seems to know everyone and has more people coming to say hello. She's obviously been away and has just come back—of course she'd hug everyone. They're probably her childhood friends, for Christ's sake.

Fuck me.

I'm being ridiculous. I turn around and walk toward the

back. I need to get out of this room, to get away from her and stop fucking staring at her.

I stalk to the back of the room, weaving between people and finally making it to the narrow door that says "Staff Only". I push it open and step through, closing it behind me with a slam. I slump onto my office chair and put my head in my hands.

This isn't me.

Women don't have that effect on me. Jealous? Of some redneck country boy? Over some woman I literally don't even know?

This isn't why I came here. I came here to get away from New York, to get away from my family's business and try to start something for myself. I didn't come here to get involved with anyone in this tiny town.

I need to get a grip. I take a couple deep breaths and blow all the air out of my lungs. There's a stack of invoices next to my computer that need to be sorted, so I pick up the first one and fire up my laptop. Nothing like some boring old numbers to cool me down after... whatever it was that just happened to me out there.

You can get the full version of Knocked Up Again by copying this link into your browser:
https://www.amazon.com/dp/B07MPCHQCB

Don't forget, you can get exclusive access to bonus chapters for ALL my books.
https://www.lilianmonroe.com/subscribe

ALSO BY LILIAN MONROE

For all books, visit:

www.lilianmonroe.com

Brother's Best Friend Romance

Shouldn't Want You

Military Romance

His Vow

His Oath

His Word

The Complete Protector Series

Enemies to Lovers Romance

Hate at First Sight

Loathe at First Sight

Despise at First Sight

Secret Baby Romance:

Knocked Up by the CEO

Knocked Up by the Single Dad

Knocked Up... Again!

Knocked Up By the Billionaire's Son

The Complete Knocked Up Series

Knocked Up by Prince Charming

Knocked Up by Prince Dashing

Knocked Up by Prince Gallant

Knocked Up by the Broken Prince

Knocked Up by the Wicked Prince

Knocked Up by the Wrong Prince

Fake Engagement/ Fake Marriage Romance:

Engaged to Mr. Right

Engaged to Mr. Wrong

Engaged to Mr. Perfect

Mr Right: The Complete Fake Engagement Series

Mountain Man Romance:

Lie to Me

Swear to Me

Run to Me

The Complete Clarke Brothers Series

Extra-Steamy Rock Star Romance:

Garrett

Maddox

Carter

The Complete Rock Hard Series

Sexy Doctors:

Doctor O

Doctor D

Doctor L

The Complete Doctor's Orders Series

Time Travel Romance:

The Cause

A little something different:

Second Chance: A Rockstar Romance in North Korea

Printed in Great Britain
by Amazon